AUNT CLARA'S SECRETS

AUNT CLARA'S SECRETS

K. J. McCALL

JJ Publishers, LLC

Published by
JJ Publishers, LLC

11445 Weatherstone Dr.
Waynesboro, Pa. 17268

www.KJMcCall.com

Printed in the United States of America

Cover by Rick Holland, myvisionpress.com

Library of Congress Control Number: 2021914595

ISBN: 978-1-7375553-0-8

One

Grace Dawson   May, 1951

This is what happened. I was barely seventeen and Aunt Clara only thirty the day she dropped two bombshells on me from her hospital bed and then died like she planned it that way. She grabbed my wrist, pulled me to her with surprising strength and whispered, "I have two things to tell you."

I smiled, expecting her secret for nutmeg pie or maybe fried chicken. That woman could fry a chicken.

"It's nothing good."

Something in her eyes gave me goosebumps. I dropped the smile.

"You'll think less of me but I have to tell somebody."

"Okay."

"You have a cousin."

"Uh …"

"A little boy. I called him Avery. Not sure what they call him now."

"What do you mean? Where is he?"

"A boy in my class … Henry is his name. It might be him. The minute he walked in, I wondered. Such a sweet little boy."

"I don't understand."

Aunt Clara shook her head, placed an icy finger across my mouth. "And the other thing … the other thing … William killed Donnie Ray Carr, pushed him down the break of the mountain."

"William?"

"I never told anybody in all this time, promised him I wouldn't."

"William who, Aunt Clara?" I was trying desperately to catch up.

"Find my little boy, Gracie. He's seven now, seven-and-a-half. Might be the one in my class, I just don't know. See if it is and, see he's all right."

"Aunt Clara, who are you talking about?" My father's name is William. Surely, she didn't mean him.

"I tried once to find out. They wouldn't tell me. In case he ever comes looking for me … tell him I'm sorry."

"William who, Aunt Clara?"

"Norton Train Station, September 1943." It was the only thing else she'd say, repeating it over and over, breathless. She loosened her grip and sank back on the pillow, exhausted from all those words.

I ran into the hall hoping for a familiar face, someone else to hear it and rescue me from being the only witness. I called for a nurse who came at a run. Not that there was any rush. During my short absence, Aunt Clara quit life.

Didn't know what to do. Tell my mother? Reject the whole thing? There it was, my biggest problem already. Nobody but me to decide. I thought then, and still think, she intended it that way, stalling like she did until everybody else had left the room.

Mother would have rejected it all as confused ramblings, but there was nothing wrong with Aunt Clara's mind. The doctor had put her in the hospital because of an infection. She'd gotten so thin, he feared her too weak to fight it on her own. Guess he was right.

Indecision caused me to say nothing at first, passed up a dozen chances at home to tell Mother. But I had to tell her sometime and the longer I put it off, the worse it would be for me. I struggled with it for three whole days and finally told her about the child.

"You don't believe her, do you?" she asked, gaping at me. "We can't trust a single thing my sister said. Half-crazy for years, long suffering about something, we never did know what. Starved herself until it ruined her health. And when could she have had a baby? She never went anywhere long enough."

"Yes, she did, the summer I turned nine, when Dad and Uncle Charles went off to war." The summer of 1943 was a big one for me, afraid all the grown-ups in my life would disappear and never come back. I was right, at least partially. My father came back when the war ended in 1945, but not to live with us anymore. Uncle Charles decided to make a career out of the Navy. Aunt Clara returned, but she had changed.

"Oh, I remember now," Mother said, grabbing my arm. "She came back so late, the principal had to find a substitute for the entire month of September. I suppose it could be true, come to think of it. She was never the same afterward, hiding in her room of an evening, moody and unstable. But, all the nonsense about the Norton Train Station ... what could *that* mean? Did she say anything else?"

I had to lie. Couldn't possibly tell her about Donnie Ray Carr. She would pounce right on it, declare my dad the guilty William, bitter even now, years after catching him in an affair and then that nasty divorce. My father couldn't have killed Donnie Ray, I knew it in my bones. He couldn't kill anyone, except maybe Mother when she turns so petty.

It rained hard the day we buried Aunt Clara. Seems like it always rains for funerals. Here in Betula, people show up no matter the weather, no matter what they thought or said about the poor soul in the coffin. Plenty came to Aunt Clara's funeral. I imagine most of them had thought and said plenty while she lived. If they only knew.

As for her family, there weren't many. Never married, parents gone. Her brother, my Uncle Charles, was on a Navy ship somewhere, so it was just us, me and my parents, in the reserved front pew.

Sitting there between them while the preacher gave his sermon, I mulled over by myself the mysterious William. Did he still live in town? Was he here with us now? And, about the boy. Whether he sat with his mom and dad somewhere behind me, thinking of himself as merely a student when he was actually a son. I wanted to turn in my seat and scan the crowd for both. I couldn't, of course. Later, though, during the gathering, I took my eyes on a trip around the room and came up empty.

My aunt left everything to me. Wasn't much of value there, my mother quickly pointed out. Aunt Clara had earned a teacher's tiny salary, and the house she lived in belonged to Uncle Charles. Still, she had chosen me to pass it to, along with those stupefying secrets, so I wanted even more to do right by her.

Turns out, we have dozens of Williams around Betula, wouldn't be surprised if it's the most popular name for men. I wondered then if the William who supposedly killed Donnie Ray Carr was also the boy's father. Aunt Clara never actually said. It was *Officer* Donnie Ray Carr, by the way, I remember that much, his disappearance linked to third grade in my memory. Our teacher kept going out in the hall to whisper about it with the principal, related somehow to Donnie Ray, his wife's cousin's son, I think it was.

I decided to do some digging on my own. In the school library I asked Miss Rettig if she had any old copies of the Betula Bulletin. She asked how old and it seemed best to just tell her what I wanted. She had to hunt for them in the back stacks, came out carrying a small armful and said they were still around only because of their historical importance to the town. She handed them over letting her curiosity show. I mumbled something about a project.

The newspapers dated back to April, 1943.

> Officer Donnie Ray Carr, 26, not seen since Friday afternoon … no signs of him or his motorcycle … anyone with information should contact the police…

> Chief Emmet Sayer says he has no leads … Chief Emmet Sayer remains optimistic … Chief Emmet Sayer refused to comment about his lack of progress.

It was front-page news for days and days until four men escaped from Alcatraz Penitentiary and knocked it to second.

Chief Sayer is still the police chief here in Betula, still an imposing figure. To everybody in town he'll always be Chief, except to my boyfriend, Obie, who calls him dear old dad. Seems I ought to have a special name to call him, but I just say Chief like everyone else. He's never suggested I call him anything different, although he often calls me Freckles, which I consider pretty chummy.

About Obie. His full name is Oliver Barrett Sayer. Seems a bit too studious for him, so we just call him Obie. He's the tallest guy in school and star of the basketball team. Mother says he's lanky.

Nobody ever figured out what happened to Donnie Ray Carr but speculation ran on for years. Some said he skipped town and moved to Florida, which seems unlikely for a cop. Some even went to murder in their thinking, though they never found a body. He and his motorcycle just disappeared one day. If I'm to believe my Aunt Clara, he's at the bottom of the break.

Mr. Grant says Betula was named after a class of tree growing thick on these hills. And he says the break of the mountain is relatively new—in Earth time, only a few thousand years. He ought to know, being the science teacher.

But some say they can remember a time when the break wasn't there, when folks in Betula could hike or ride horseback over the mountain to Eugene, Kentucky on the other side. Some say they can remember barroom fights about who owned the mountaintop, Virginians or Kentuckians. And some claim to remember the very night it split. The gosh-awfulest storm they ever saw—downed trees, blown-away roofs, thunder loud enough to bust eardrums, lightning flashes that turned night into day. They insist the break in the mountain was a result, as though God wanted to forever mark the boundary so everyone would know. Mr. Grant says these stories are mostly myth.

They say, after the storm, the break was only a few inches wide. A person could still cross over the mountain that way just by stepping over it, easy as pie. Mr. Grant says it cannot be true, and I can tell you it's never been done in my memory. It is wide enough now that nobody ever thinks of stepping over it or jumping it, not even my daredevil friends. You cannot see bottom, so you know it's a long way. Trees and bushes spring out from the rock wall on both sides. If you're up there looking down, all you see is green. Even with the winter snows you can still see some green. Warmer down there, I suppose, nearer to the center of the earth. I bet Mr. Grant is closer to correct. The break looks permanent to me, as though it happened eons ago.

Nobody knows for sure where the boundary is up there, and does it really matter? Betula and Eugene are now joined by a twenty-minute stretch of road, Highway 21. We live on that road, Mother and me, near the state line. As a child, I liked to straddle the line with one foot in Virginia, the other in Kentucky. It seemed like an amazing feat to me. Silly kid.

Don't know how it was back then, but the break belongs to us nowadays, me and my friends. They say the Kentucky side is not particularly accessible, but on the Virginia side we can drive right up on an old logging road. We go there in the summer to picnic and party and drink beer. Some go up at night to neck. I refuse to do that though, not me, not there. What if Officer Reed were to catch us or, heaven forbid, Chief Sayer himself. He's been known to show up after dark with a flashlight and bad attitude.

We're not the first to claim the break, judging from all the initials carved on trees. Kids like us have been going there forever, maybe even the Chief when he was seventeen. Anymore though, I can't be up there without thinking of the bottom and Donnie Ray Carr.

Others have vanished over the years. Elwood Purdy, for one, the town drunk everybody hated because he ran over and killed the mayor's little girl. And another man, too. Can't remember his name, started with a G. People hated him because of his routine—got paid on Friday, drank it up on Saturday, spent Sunday whipping his wife and son and their poor little dog. It was the same every weekend until he suddenly wasn't around to do it anymore. Nobody knows what happened to either of those men and there hasn't been much interest in finding out. Some say it was mountain justice—these mountains took them because they were so bad.

But, there was plenty of interest in what happened to Donnie Ray Carr. And here, Aunt Clara supposedly knew all along. Now that she's gone, maybe I'm the only one, me and the guilty. Of course, I don't really *know* anything but the idea gives me goosebumps all the same.

Two

I wanted so much to tell Obie but didn't see how, not until I knew which William. I'd have to swear him to secrecy, especially with his father, and that wouldn't be fair. They butt heads sometimes and Obie often complains, but he adores the man and wants to be just like him. He *is* like him already – same way of walking, same measure of right and wrong, same nose for puzzles. And he hopes to be Chief Sayer himself one day.

I did tell him about the alleged baby, however, which gave him enough to chew on. We both agreed a trip to the Norton Train Station was the only thing to be done, so I decided to go on my first free Saturday. Didn't say anything to Mother, merely attended to the clocks and left the house. I've been winding the clock in the kitchen and the one on the mantle every Saturday morning since I was tall enough to reach them standing on a chair. It was an event back then.

Obie dropped me off at our train station in the drizzle. Well, we don't have an actual station in Betula, more a shed with a ticket window on a splintery wood platform. We're a tiny stop on the L&N Railroad, built by the mining company to haul out coal. Coal is pretty big here, in case you don't know. If it weren't for the coal, I doubt there'd be a train or the tracks for it to run on.

Under an umbrella, I waited on the platform twenty minutes. As the train approached, my feet knew it first. I climbed aboard and had my pick of seats. Rain messed up the view out the window, the clouded-over sun gave no hint of direction but I knew it to be southwest. We'd been to Norton a few times before, and when we went it was considered a big deal. Norton is twice as big as Betula (which isn't saying much), with a movie theater, a JC Penney, and an actual train station you can walk around in, buy a snack, get out of the weather.

It took about forty minutes to get there. I stood at the station entrance wondering what this squared-off building could possibly reveal. There were pictures on the walls, so I strolled around, stopped in front of each one. All of them were of trains. I went to the ticket window, stared at a man in horn-rimmed glasses trying to think of something to ask. "Good morning, I was just wondering … uh, never mind, sorry." Why this train station? Was the boy born here? Something must have happened but no sign of it now. I bought a candy bar and a bottle of pop, then walked around some more. Back to the window. "Can you tell me how to get to the newspaper office?"

"Three blocks down," he said, "on the left."

At the Norton Gazette, the man behind the counter looked a lot like my science teacher. "Is there a way to find out about something that happened here in Norton in September of 1943?"

"Can you be more specific?" He didn't sound like Mr. Grant at all. "I mean, we had the war in 1943 so a lot of things happened."

"Had to do with a baby."

"Babies are born, babies die—news enough around here to make the paper, even in a war. Oh, wait. They found a baby at the train station once, somebody left it there. Might have been about that time."

"Please, no!" I whispered.

"Beg your pardon?"

I took a deep breath, and then another. "Sorry, nothing. Do you keep copies that old?"

"We have all our newspapers, back as far as 1919. Finding the exact one might be a problem in other news offices but we keep our stacks fairly well ordered," he said with obvious pride. "I'll take you down if you promise to leave them that way."

I promised.

The stairs were dark with a low ceiling. He turned on a light at the top and had to duck his head going down. At the bottom he tugged on a chain to turn on another light, then cleared a table and found me a chair. "During the war, we published a daily paper so you will have plenty to look at. Summer of '43, you say?"

"No, just September."

"Oh, well, one month shouldn't be too bad." He led me into a narrow aisle, touching piles of yellowed papers as he went. "Okay, this is '43, December … November …

October … here it is, September. I'll carry half over to the table for you. If you don't find anything, you can come back for the other half. All right?"

"Okay, thanks."

"If it's about the abandoned baby it won't be hard. Something like that would be front page and above the fold for several days unless big war news beat it out."

I went through the first pile quickly, glancing only at the main headline in each. Then I went back to the other pile and began leafing through them on the shelf. I soon found it. Front-page headline on the issue dated September 18, 1943:

Baby Abandoned Yesterday in Train Station

And the September 19 issue:

Search for Mother of Train Station Baby

A boy, healthy and well fed … appeals for information … search for the mother … a young woman reported a baby left on a bench and then took a train for points east … speculation she might be the mother … fruitless search … baby turned over to Wise County Children's Home.

I put all the newspapers back on the shelf and camped at the table in confusion. The woman who did this was foreign to me. I could more easily picture my Aunt Clara robbing a bank. But I had to face facts, it had to be her. She must have been desperate, was all I could say.

"Where's the Wise County Children's Home?" I asked upstairs.

"Did you put the papers back like you found them?"

"Yes, Sir."

"Okay, good. It's out on Dorchester Road. Did you find something?"

"Can I walk there?"

"Well, it's a couple or three miles," he said, picking up fast that I didn't want to talk about it. "Taxi might be better. The taxi stand's across the street and a block down. Burt can run you out there in a jiffy and it won't cost much, probably about fifty cents." He leaned in and whispered, "Have you got the fare?" Gosh, what a nice man.

>*>*>*<*<*<

I smiled at a woman with salt-and-pepper hair at the Wise County Children's Home, assuming she'd be as nice as Burt and the newspaper man. She wasn't.

"One moment, please." She spoke without looking up, and then continued to read the page in front of her for what seemed like a long time. Nothing for me to do except stand there nervously and wrap hair around my finger. "Are you the pregnant girl from Duffield?" she finally asked, inspecting first my middle and then the rest of me.

"Uh, no."

"Then, who are you?"

"I'd like to inquire about a baby."

"Yes?"

I quickly summed up the newspaper articles. "The last one said they brought the baby here."

"Why are you asking? You're too young to be the mother. You're the second one come about that baby in as many months. After … how many years has it been now. Seven? Yes, after a space of over seven years, we've got two finally come to ask questions about that poor little boy." She glared at me with pursed lips.

"Somebody else came?"

She gave me a vigorous nod. "And this one was the mother, I'm certain. Although she didn't admit it. I should have called the police to have her arrested for abandonment."

I pulled out a photograph of Aunt Clara. "Is this her?"

"Is this *she*, you mean. Yes, that's the one. And who are you?"

"Grace Dawson. She's my Aunt Clara, or she was. She died recently." A look of satisfaction came up on the woman's face. I'm not kidding! She didn't even try to hide it. "Did she have the baby here?" I asked, trying to keep my composure.

"We are an adoption agency, not a home for unwed mothers. She had it somewhere else, I don't know where, and then left the poor thing in the train station, of all places."

"I'm trying to find out what happened to the baby and who the father was."

"The baby was adopted out years ago. It's what we do here with abandoned children. Nothing came with that baby, no information whatsoever, so we don't know anything about the parents."

"Oh," I said, dejected.

She softened a little bit around the eyes. No help for her mouth, however, circled by permanent crimps from pursing her lips all the time. "You need the birth certificate. It'll tell you who the father was, when and where the baby was born."

"The birth certificate, of course! I hadn't thought of that. You don't have it, I guess."

"I already told you we got no information!" She took a deep breath and let it out with a sigh. "Look, Miss ..."

"Dawson."

"The mother must have kept it. You should try to find it. If you do, we'd appreciate seeing it to update the file." She looked at me hard. "If your Aunt Clara was the mother, then the baby is your cousin. And right now, your little cousin's file is marked 'unidentified'. Are you happy with that?"

I walked out of there feeling Aunt Clara's guilt. It hung like a cloud over my head as dense as the ones in the sky. I managed to shake it off on the train ride home, but a sorry truth stuck: The search for my little cousin would hit a stone wall without that birth certificate.

Three

Aunt Clara had lived in the house on Smoketown Road her whole life, lived there alone since the day the Judge died. If the birth certificate still existed, that's where it would be. The house is a rambling place filled with books, antiques and dust, always dark and gloomy, even on a sunny day, because of the drapes, all the trees in the yard and the over-grown rhododendron at the windows.

The Judge has been dead three years and I still feel his stern and silent presence in there. He would always be "the Judge" to me. I cannot remember hearing him called anything else. Not ever. Not by his wife or even his own kids. I was his only grandchild and couldn't imagine calling him Gramps.

According to my mother, her mother got sick and died on purpose just to escape him. She still resents the sweet old lady for running out, but I don't know why. The Judge became Aunt Clara's problem after Grandmother died. I remember my aunt trying to soften him from the kitchen with his favorite cream pies and fried chicken. I never saw a sign that it worked, though, and if her cooking didn't do it, nothing would.

Frankly, I did not want to go into that house by myself. Since Aunt Clara's death I'd been there only once, and it was with Mother. Obie agreed to come with me on the birth certificate search. Nobody else seemed interested in the house or its contents, viewing it as merely the home of dull old Clara Bond. But none of them had heard what I heard or knew what I knew. Not even Obie had heard all of it. And Mother, who still didn't know about the trip to Norton, was in for a surprise. Aunt Clara had been the old-maid school teacher everybody pitied. Always sad and nobody knew why, never married and nobody knew why, starved herself into an early grave and nobody would ever know why. Unless I told them.

As Obie and I stood in the front hall with flashlights, Aunt Clara seemed more of a puzzle to me than ever, her past so deep and mysterious.

It was his first time to be in the biggest house in town. "I know your Uncle Charles owns this place but how about everything in it? Is it all yours?" he asked, looking around.

"Beats me."

"This is exciting, don't you think?" He nudged my shoulder and tugged my hair. "We're searching for the birth certificate but you never can tell what else we might find." Obie's optimism on display, one of the million things I love about him.

We rolled back the heavy pocket doors to the Judge's library and peeked in from where we stood. I'd never actually been in the room, never seen more of it than we were seeing then. It had a dusty, undisturbed look.

"Shouldn't we check in here?" Obie nodded toward the mammoth desk and the safe on the wall.

"Everything's probably locked. Besides, I doubt Aunt Clara ever went in there. Nobody did but the Judge."

"Oh," he said, disappointed, as we dragged the doors back shut.

Where to start. We looked in all the obvious places first. Aunt Clara's desk collected dust by a window in the parlor, compact and square with spindly legs, fragile compared to the Judge's. It was unlocked and waiting, we went through every drawer. A rich-looking carved box held letters from Uncle Charles. I thumbed through them just to be sure. Paintings on the walls, a vase the size of a butter churn in a corner of the floor, smaller vases on tables, more on shelves. Were they all mine now? Were they worth anything? We peeked behind the paintings for another safe, found nothing but wall.

Like any teacher, Aunt Clara had accumulated books, lots of books. We started in on them, looking at each one separately, fanning through it to see if anything fell out. She'd formed the habit of hiding things in books—cards, letters, that sort of thing, even some cash in small bills. I put them in a pile to go through later. But no birth certificate.

Upstairs, we stayed clear of the Judge's end of the hall. Mother's old room seemed sparse. She'd taken much of it, little by little, over the years—books, pictures, even some furniture. Uncle Charles's room hadn't changed since the war.

The bureau clock in Aunt Clara's bedroom had run down, same as the rest of the clocks in the house. It seemed right to just to leave them all that way. I'd often been in my aunt's bedroom, but part of me dreaded what we might find there. And it felt odd, this after-death meddling into her private things. I'm sure Obie felt it worse, the way he half-heartedly checked her closet, pulling boxes from a tall shelf to look in. Soon, he closed the closet door with a sigh and muttered, "Nothing in those boxes except hats and shoes."

But what he did next was all that mattered. It led to the prize. He bent down to look under the bed and found her old suitcase, simple as pie. Disturbing dust, he dragged it out and plunked it onto Aunt Clara's lacy bedspread. We stared at it.

Prickles came up on my arms. I knew we'd find the birth certificate in there, I could feel it. "Gosh, Obie, this might be the one she took away with her."

"It's locked. Want me to break it?"

"Wait, I saw keys in the jewelry chest." There seemed to be no shortage of keys. Several appeared to be about the right size and I handed them to him. The first two did not work at all. The third one fit but he had to jiggle it. The suitcase smelled musty inside, like something smells when it's been shut up a long time. Yellowed newspapers, her own private writings in journals with frayed corners, and a Bible.

"Hey, a Bible," Obie said. "Could be in there. People always keep important stuff in Bibles."

I picked it up and fanned through it. A single sheet of paper, folded once, floated onto the bed from somewhere in the New Testament. I opened it flat and we both laughed out loud.

Certificate of Birth
State of Kentucky

Date of Birth: September 11, 1943
Full Name: William Avery Dollarhide, Jr.
Mother: Clara Anne Bond
Father: William Avery Dollarhide
Place of Birth: Louisville, Kentucky

Obie grabbed it out of my hands. "Damn, Gracie! Do you see who the father is?"

It didn't register at first. I only cared it wasn't *my* father. "William Avery Dollarhide ... is that ... Bill Dollarhide?"

"One and the same, our very own state senator. He wasn't a senator yet, but still ..."

"Holy moley! Bill Dollarhide!" Everybody knew Senator Dollarhide. He was the top of the heap. Not only our state senator, but part of the Capshaw Foundry empire and you don't get any higher in Betula. "But, how could it have happened? He's married to Howard Capshaw's daughter."

"Doesn't surprise me. Stuff like that happens all the time," Obie said with a knowing nod.

My Aunt Clara with a married man? Didn't seem possible. And he was tremendously handsome, a lot like Kirk Douglas right down to the chin dimple. I couldn't picture my dowdy aunt with him. Although, in photographs taken back then she looked different. People say I resemble her when she was my age, which might be a compliment because she looked pretty good.

It suddenly dawned on me. If William Avery Dollarhide was the father, then William Avery Dollarhide killed Donnie Ray Carr! Unless Aunt Clara meant two different Williams, and what was the chance of that. I paced around excitedly, bounced on the balls of my feet. I couldn't help it! "Obie," I said, grabbing his arm. "Aunt Clara told me something else the day she died, something besides the baby."

"What?"

I told him.

"Do you realize what you're saying? Dollarhide is just about the most important man in town, the head cheese, and you're accusing him of killing a cop!"

"I'm not accusing him. Aunt Clara accused him."

"Yeah, and she's gone. We don't actually know if she witnessed it. And we don't know for sure which William she was talking about."

"Sure, we know. We have the birth certificate."

"Technically, we don't have proof that they are the same William."

"Don't be ridiculous, Obie. Of course, it's the same. Aunt Clara told me two things that day. At the time, I wasn't sure whether to believe her. But now, knowing the first one's true, it gives me a lot more reason to believe in the other. She didn't give me the name of the *father*, she gave me the name of the *killer*. She said, and I quote, William killed Donnie Ray Carr."

"And that's another thing. All we have is you saying she said it."

22

"Don't you believe me?

"Of course, I believe you."

"Don't you believe he did it?"

"Yes, but it doesn't matter what I believe."

"Aren't you going to tell your father?"

"Of course, I'll tell him, I have to tell him. But he's gonna be shocked and I'm just preparing you for what he'll say. I remember when Donnie Ray disappeared. Pop was never home that entire spring, missed all my softball practices. He struggled without a deputy for months until he finally decided Donnie Ray was gone for good. Then he couldn't find a replacement because everybody decent had gone to war. Pop said Donnie Ray was the best this town had to offer when it came to police work, and he wasn't around to solve his own case."

Obie took me home with him to see his father that same evening. The Chief always appears less fierce settled in an armchair and without a uniform. He smiles more, and when he smiles his eyes get involved. Just like Obie's.

When I showed the Chief the birth certificate he looked confused at first, then said, "Jesus," and whistled through his teeth.

I told him what all Aunt Clara had said the day she died, trying to recall it exactly.

He whistled through his teeth twice. "I always figured Dollarhide did it. Never trusted the man, and Donnie Ray was investigating him on a graft charge at the time."

"What's a graft charge?" I asked.

23

"Fraudulent use of his position."

"Gosh, that can't be a coincidence."

"We questioned him extensively. Didn't lead us anywhere, even the graft charges fell through. We couldn't pin a thing on him."

"Yeah, but what about now, after hearing what Aunt Clara said?"

"I can see how worked up you are about this, Grace, but a woman's dying declaration is not worth much."

"You couldn't … reopen the case?"

"No, I'd need a lot more than that."

"Like what? What all would you need?"

"A body, for starters. A weapon."

"But, Aunt Clara said William pushed Donnie Ray down the break."

"Well, that's that, then."

"What do you mean?"

"It's like saying he … pushed him off the planet. No retrieving a body from down there, especially after this much time. Even if we could trudge in and find a body, we would need some evidence to tie Dollarhide to it. Maybe it was an accident and the best we'd get would be manslaughter. Hell, excuse me Grace, for all we know, your Aunt Clara pushed him down there herself, since she's the one who knew about it. That's what a good defense attorney would say."

His dose of reality punched a hole in our enthusiasm and we sat there in silence. I twisted hair around my index finger and thought about it, not quite accepting it as the end. We were supposed to find the birth certificate. The search had been too easy, the location too pat to believe anything else.

Obie went into the kitchen, came back eating an apple and tossed one to me. "Pop, is it all right if we poke around in Donnie Ray's old files, anyway?"

"Sure, son, go ahead. No, wait. Do you have time for it? Have you finished that term paper?"

"Uh, I'm working on it."

"Well, set your attention on ancient Troy and get it done. Then you can poke around in the files."

Obie does not care much about school. He half-heartedly works at it just to please his parents, which I view as a fine thing. His father says college will be the making of him, but Obie would rather go into police work right here in Betula. Obie's older brother, Caleb, the studious one, had died in the war. Six years have passed since it happened and the family is still raw. They rarely speak of Caleb, but he's still around. Teachers compare, expecting more. And Obie worries his dad will always measure him by the Caleb yardstick when it comes to school.

My father says Obie makes up for his disinterest in book learning with a flair toward enterprise, voluntarily taking over his family's neglected orchard as a money-making venture, for example, then buying himself that used Ford truck with a good apple crop. Dad says I could do a lot worse, and he's not even taking into account Obie's blue eyes and that wide grin.

I got home and decided to tell Mother everything. She hates it when I leave her in the dark. For once, she had little to say, stunned speechless that her sister actually *did* have a child and the father was Senator William Avery Dollarhide, who apparently pushed Donnie Ray Carr down the break.

Four

We went to the library after school the next day so Obie could research the ancient city of Troy. My term paper was already finished and handed in, freeing me up to focus on the boy in Aunt Clara's class. Was he her son? I figured the answer would be easy to find if he wasn't, not so easy if he was.

She'd said his name was Henry. I looked on the second grade page in the yearbook and saw two—Henry Cane and Henry Mullin. And, believe it or not, Henry Mullin had a chin dimple! Well, that was enough for me. Obie said I was making things too simple, and maybe I was, but didn't that mean it was him?

There were two Mullin listings in the telephone book and I knew one of them—Harriett Mullin over on Cherry Lane. She didn't have a brother, so it had to be the one on Decatur Rd.

Before I tell you about going over there, I need to tell you about my car, a green Chevy coupe my father bought new. Mother said he was just trying to buy my love. But, why would he do that, I asked, when he already had plenty.

Anyway, I drove myself across town to Decatur Road, working on an excuse to knock on the Mullin's door and start a conversation that would somehow lead to the big question: Did you adopt your son?

Over there, I remembered being on the same street once before. Abby Harding lived up the block on the left, and in eighth grade she had a slumber party I'll never forget. It was the night Susie Frasier, with a nasty snicker, called me "funny looking" in front of the other girls. They said it was just jealousy because she had a crush on Obie and he was partial to me even then. But I still can't pass a mirror without staring into it and wondering. Obie tells me I'm cute all the time, "your dark brown eyes and cute-as-a-button nose," he says. Except, he could be talking about Frosty the Snowman with a description like that.

Nowadays, Susie probably says even worse about me since she evidently still has her cap set. Well, I said back then, and I'm still saying, she can just find another dream because Obie belongs to me. I wear his class ring on a chain around my neck and I never take it off, not even to take a bath. My only real competition is the four-legged kind, Buster and Old Blue. Not sure of their exact breed but, like most dogs around here, they are hounds.

From the way it looked, a hundred kids lived on Decatur Road and they were all playing outside. I found the Mullin house, a tired little place in sore need of paint. And I spotted Henry, too, or thought I did—a cute little guy with droopy socks and a band-aid on his knee. One look at him made me feel my lack of family. I wanted this boy for a cousin.

Since no decent excuse had surfaced to visit Mrs. Mullin, I decided to drop in on Abby instead. When I rang the bell,

Mrs. Harding appeared at the door in a flowered dress like one my mother wears. "Oh, Grace honey, bless your heart! I am so sorry about your Aunt Clara. You all right? How's your mother?"

"Okay, we're both okay." She and Mother are about the same age, went to school together in this small town, so of course they know each other. Mother says Mrs. Harding has a talent for holding a conversation all by herself, so I didn't worry overmuch about an excuse to visit.

"Abigail isn't home right now but come in anyway and have a seat here on the porch. I'll go get us some iced tea." She soon came back with the tea and a plate of cookies on a tray. "You're pretty as a picture," she said, not looking at me. "Well, tell me … how've you been? Have you got your prom dress yet? No? Better get it soon before they are all picked over. I took Abigail to buy hers last Saturday and it plumb wore me out. She must have tried on every long dress in town and finally settled on the blue one in the Mercantile window. Know the one I mean? Hope you didn't have your heart set on it. They peeled it right off so Abby could try it on. In broad daylight, mind! I liketa died. That plastic statue was still standing naked when we left. There oughta be a law."

I nibbled an iced snickerdoodle, spooned sugar into my tea and stirred longer than necessary while she described her husband's backaches and the flowers in the yard. She talked on and on with no interference from me and I freely admit to a wandering mind. Then I found her staring at me like it was my turn to talk, and I had to say, "I'm sorry, what?"

"I said, what can you tell me about Abigail's boyfriend, Ralph?"

All I could do was stutter at first because she'd caught me off my guard. I mean, Ralph is okay, but he's no world prize. He's a chubby egghead who wants to be a nuclear physicist.

"Is he nice?" Mrs. Hardin asked, trying to prompt me.

"Oh, yes, he's very nice, and he's gentlemanly."

"But, is he popular? Is he good enough for my Abby? He isn't very attractive."

Ah, geez. "Well, he's not the most popular boy in school, but he's really smart. Mr. Grant says he's got a bright future." That seemed to satisfy her. The truth is, Ralph makes a good match for Abby who's always had a big brain herself, and no boyfriends. "How is your son?" I finally squeezed in. "Is he playing out there somewhere?"

"Across the street, the one with the copper-colored hair. See him roughhousing with the rest? If there's a pile of boys, he'll be in the middle of it."

"How old is he now?"

"Eleven last month, and he's springing up like mad. Outgrew all his pants and—"

"Who's the little boy with the blond hair and red shirt?"

"Henry Mullin. Isn't he a dear? Would you believe he is adopted? Told me so himself."

Bingo! I couldn't help smiling.

"I think it's wise when parents tell a child the truth. Don't you? They moved into town just last year from Big Stone Gap, then his adoptive father suddenly died. A problem with his heart, they said. Poor little guy. Imagine being rejected by your real parents and then losing a father again. His mother had to go to work. The lady next door keeps an eye on him so it's okay for now, but sounds like money is a problem."

It isn't especially nice, but I had trouble sitting still after that. The rest of what she said barely registered, eager as I was to get away and tell Obie, my eyes on the porch steps. I said goodbye feeling pretty decent, though, about the whole thing. I got what I came for and Mrs. Harding got to sit on her shady porch and talk. Not a bad trade. The cookies are my only regret. Lost track of the exact number but I think it was five. I know, I know. It's just that I tend to eat more when I'm fidgety.

Obie said finding the boy was good sleuthing or maybe just coincidence. I would have bet my car on it, but in his opinion we still didn't know for sure whether this adopted boy was Aunt Clara's.

However, something of a more personal and pressing nature was on my mind right then. The mention of Abby's prom dress reminded me of my own serious lack. Mother said my Homecoming dress from last October would be good enough. I'd only worn it once, dresses were expensive, etc. But, oh, oh, oh! I wanted something new. My father solved the problem, as usual. He gave me a fold of money and told me to get what I want.

I need to tell you about my father. For one thing, he's a lawyer. Have I mentioned that? It's what I want to be someday, part of a fuzzy future Obie and I have planned, where he'll round up the criminals and I'll put them away. Dad is a major source of wisdom for me, even if he did cheat on Mother way back when. These days he's solid and honest, stays out of other folks' business and warns me to do the same. Although, staying out of other folks' business seems contrary to practicing law.

Dad owns a car and a motorcycle, which Mother calls excessive. He's a sucker for new inventions and supports the modern age. Even bought himself a television that takes up half his living room, and a pop-up toaster, practically the first one in town. Mother won't let either of them into our house. She says the toaster is an extravagance when you've got an oven, the television a silly fad that'll fade. And she fears they both might explode. Don't want you to think I'm deprived, though. I have a nice radio and a record player with a growing collection of hit records.

And just last year, Dad bought us a washing machine. Then he replaced our icebox with a new refrigerator, which meant a permanent end to ice blocks and catch pans. Mother doesn't seem to fear either of these things or view them extravagant.

I had already told Dad what all Aunt Clara said the day she died, and I shared the rest over meatloaf and mashed potatoes at the diner in town. William Dollarhide's name on the birth certificate turned his face slightly red and prompted him to utter, "That man is a lowlife, I've suspected it for years."

But when he realized the man had almost certainly pushed Donnie Ray Carr into the break, my easy-going dad sloshed his beer and then cracked his plate by dropping a knife down too hard on it.

A waitress came to take the plate away and wipe gravy off the table. By the time she finished, he'd composed himself enough to boil the situation down to two things. Number one, Dollarhide needed to go to prison. Number two, nothing I could contribute would help put him there.

How frustrating to know the truth and not be able to prove it. I had no earthly idea what to do next. Turned out, Mother was the one to tell me. She walked into my bedroom and said, "I've been thinking. Clara always wrote in a book. Not so much the last few years, but earlier. Everything that happened, everything she thought and did. I can't believe all this stuff happened and she didn't write it down."

"We did see some old journals in the suitcase. I thumbed through one of them from the late 1930s. Definitely her handwriting."

"Like I said, if this stuff really happened, and I'm not saying it did, she would have scribbled it down somewhere. Might be worth another look."

So, I paid a second visit to Aunt Clara's suitcase. There were eleven journals in all, dating from the mid 30's to 1943. The yellowed newspaper articles we ignored the first time were a quick read this time. They explained a lot, in themselves. I brought the journals back with me and snuck them into the house. Then later, after Mother had gone to bed, I fixed myself a bowl of cornbread and milk and read through them one by one. The earlier journals didn't matter much but the last one, the one from 1943?

Pure gold. Thank you, Mother.

Five

Journal of Clara Bond, 1943

Thursday, April 29

What should I do? Dear God, what should I do? William trusts me not to tell. I promised him I wouldn't, and I won't. Such a horrible secret, though. Can I just let it slide?

I need to think of my own pressing problem now. He trusts me to stay quiet for him; I must trust him to come through for me. But he was so cold, so angry when I told him about the baby. It was just the shock. At least I had a time of suspicion before I knew. He had no warning at all, just the words, "I'm going to have a baby," without a thought of it the moment before. My fault, really. I actually believed he'd be happy about it. Seems ridiculous now. He said he would take care of me, but I doubt he sees the urgency. We must get married soon or everyone will know. Plus, he's leaving for Camp Forrest any minute, so it has to be now.

Monday, May 10

Still waiting to hear from William. I have listened for the telephone and the doorbell, stared out the window each evening, hoping he'd come. I went to his office twice. Always in a meeting. Avoidance and a stall. That's his game, I guess. Stalling through all my attempts to convince, giving me hope with his pretty-sounding words and silky voice. The Judge says William is a wolf in wolf's clothing and I'm a fool not to see it. Maybe he's right. Yesterday was Mother's Day. Gracie gave Evelyn a little bracelet I helped her pick out.

Monday, May 24

Finally, a letter. Apology for not being able to get away just now, and two hundred in cash. After some clandestine library research on homes for unwed mothers, I have chosen the Salvation Army Home in Louisville, Kentucky. Far enough away, and the train out of Norton goes right there without a transfer. In a carefully worded reply, I told him my plan and where I'll be, giving him every chance.

Thursday, June 10

I am all business now. No other choice, no more time for emotions. Nearly six months gone and showing. It's okay at home because nobody notices me. At school, an art smock helps. I put it on in the classroom, forget to take it off, and I'm with children all day. Though, in the lunchroom today I heard a sharp-eyed teacher whisper, "I think Clara Bond is putting on weight." Good hearing can be a curse sometimes.

The timing is right, at least. Summer vacation begins in a week—leave town at the start, return at the end. Simple enough. And it must be adoption. I can't come back with a baby, unmarried still. Not possible for a schoolteacher, and the Judge's daughter, to boot. I've been talking about going back to Radford College for the summer, to take courses toward a master's degree.

Saturday, June 19

School let out Wednesday for the summer and I'm wasting no time. Yesterday I caught the train to Norton and, instead of going east to Radford, I bought a ticket west to Louisville, 287 railroad miles. Plenty of time to think, yet nothing else, really, to decide.

I checked into a Louisville hotel last night and shopped in town today. Bought a little yellow layette for the baby. Somehow, I feel better knowing he or she will be well turned out to meet the new parents. I'm staying in the hotel again tonight, dreading and fearing the Home.

I'll have to face it tomorrow.

Sunday, June 20

It rained this morning on the taxi ride. When I got there, a woman took me to a room with four beds and three other girls, on the second floor. Everybody I saw looked like a kid. At twenty-two, I seem to be the oldest.

Right away, the woman gave me adoption papers to sign. So I wouldn't have to deal with it later, she said. But one of the girls, Marsha is her name, warned me against it with just a look and the smallest shake of her head. "What if you change your mind?" she explained after the woman left.

At least I'm here now, another hurdle jumped. The girls seem nice. Maybe it won't be that bad.

Wednesday, July 7

The Home isn't that bad, really. It helps to have the other girls—Marsha and Mary, both seventeen, and Ruthie, only fifteen. The four of us in room five are all due about the same time. We each have a twin bed and a locker for clothes. The bathroom is just down the hall and we have a sink in our room. There are six other rooms filled with other girls. We have chores to do. Nothing strenuous—help in the kitchen, set the tables, clean the bathrooms, run the vacuum—things like that. The rest of the time we just lounge around and talk.

An us-against-them spirit has developed amongst us; we're all in the same mess. We never mention our dreams of the future because we don't have any. This sort of thing does not happen to nice girls, so the chance at a decent life for us is pretty much over.

Nobody says we are "pregnant" and we never refer to ourselves that way. We are "expecting" or "gone" as in "five months gone." In fact, I heard the word "pregnant" only once in all this time, when the doctor in Jenkins, Kentucky confirmed my condition. "Yes, you're definitely pregnant, Mrs. Curtis," he said, using the fake name I gave him.

Part of me still believes William will show up. I picture the woman in the office coming to say I have a visitor downstairs. I want to tell the others my fantasy, to hear them laugh out loud and say, "me too!" But I never will. Such a silly notion that any man who's already escaped his fate would voluntarily enter this no-man's land.

Sunday, August 15

They say the Home is at full capacity because of the war and, yes, it seems like half the girls got into trouble with a departing soldier or sailor fighting overseas. And then there's Marsha who swears her boyfriend enlisted just to avoid her. In this house, consumed with our predicaments, it's easy to forget the war. My own William has no doubt already left for Camp Forrest, which turns my fantasy even more foolish.

We talk little of the war, and even less of "going over", a metaphor for going to the hospital to give birth. It is something we all fear and know little about. They've told us a few things, like the euphoria to expect right after the birth, followed by the depression. They say separation from the baby might be hard and we can choose to never see it, which is sometimes best. But they never tell us about the birth itself and we don't ask. We just want to be finished with it, finished with all of it.

Often at breakfast we find a girl missing and they tell us she went over last night. We don't see her again.

Thursday, September 9

For two months we have watched others go over, one by one. Then, Marsha started feeling pains at nine o'clock the other night. They took her to the infirmary to be examined, and off she went. Last night it was Ruthie.

I miss them.

Sunday morning, September 12

On Friday, my water broke. A nurse from the infirmary had to tell me because I wasn't sure. She packed me into a car and drove me to the hospital. When we got there she left the motor running, walked me in and said, "I've got another girl from the Home." She handed them my papers, then pivoted and walked away without a word. They put me in a bed and left me there alone. Nobody to hold my hand, nobody to say things would be all right. Some doctor I'd never seen before finally came to check on me.

I don't know how it is for normal mothers—delivered by the family doctor, loving husband near, and folks to visit. For those of us here, it's a lonely ordeal, one you just need to get through so you can move on. I barely remember my fits of pain and fear, except they seemed to go on forever.

I woke up in the recovery room. The clock in there said 8:15. I had been in labor only seven hours or so. They said it was quick for a first baby. A nurse was busy working on me, pushing on my stomach. It hurt. She noticed my open eyes and said in a businesslike tone, "You've had your baby."

"I had my baby?"

She didn't look at me or answer. She was just doing her job.

"What was it?"

"It was a boy."

"Oh, it was a boy." I smiled at her hoping she'd make eye contact and maybe share this important moment with me. I remember being glad it was a boy because boys don't have children. They have it better, all around. It's the girls who get pregnant and suffer, the girls who must hide or live with the shame. "Can I see him?" I asked.

"Yes, in the morning."

"Can't I see him now?"

"No. They bring the babies in at ten and at two. You'll have to wait 'til then."

They wheeled me upstairs to a room with four beds. Two were empty. The other had Ruthie Giblin in it, half asleep. She had delivered two days before. It was dark outside, maybe ten or ten-thirty by then. Ruthie woke up and gave me a weak little smile. Suddenly, I felt euphoric, happy to have it all behind me. I told Ruthie as much, assuming she felt the same. But she didn't seem happy, eyes all red from crying, so I figured her euphoric stage had ended and her depression had begun. It seemed awfully fast. I asked what was wrong.

"Oh, it's just that ... I'm going home tomorrow, which means I'll be saying goodbye to my little girl."

I was surprised at the change. We'd felt the same way just a few days ago. We were both going to give our babies a clean start, walk away wiser, make the best of our own lives. "If you feel so strongly, isn't there any way you can keep her?"

She blew her nose and pondered. "I will answer you this way. I talked to Father Ryan when I was five months gone. Don't know why I did it, guess I thought he could help. I told him the father didn't want to marry me and I asked him what I should do. Maybe I hoped he would make my boyfriend marry me. But instead, he asked if the boy was a Catholic and I said no. Then Father Ryan said it didn't matter

41

that he wouldn't marry me because, if he wasn't Catholic, we couldn't get married in the church anyhow."

"Ruthie, that's terrible."

"No, here's the terrible part. He said he couldn't baptize the baby if it was born out of wedlock. And if she wasn't baptized, she would stay in purgatory for all eternity instead of going to Heaven when she dies."

"Ruthie!"

"How do you like that? There I was, fifteen years old, messing around with the final resting place of my unborn child's soul. I started to cry. From the weight of it, I guess. He patted my hand and said all was not lost. I had options. I could marry a good Catholic man, or give the baby to a good Catholic family who could put everything right. Since I don't happen to know a good Catholic man who wants to get married, it has to be this."

"Oh, Ruthie! Do you believe all of that? About purgatory, I mean."

"To be honest, it sounded pretty good to me. Leave town for a few months and then come back as though it never happened. But, now I have seen her, now I've held her. I'm saying goodbye tomorrow because it's the only choice I have, and I just wanna die."

I felt sorry for Ruthie but couldn't relate. I had not talked to my preacher out of fear he'd tell the Judge, yet I'd never heard him mention purgatory in our Baptist church. Well, Ruthie had her reasons for doing this and I had mine. Every girl at the Home had her own set of reasons, but they were all rooted in the same two: fear of ruin and no support.

"Take my advice, Clara. Don't look at your baby too close, or hold him too much. Remember what they said about separation being hard."

"Oh, I'll be okay. I just want to see him, make sure he's all right."

"Yeah, that's what I said. Whatever you do, don't unwrap the blanket. You'll just get attached."

Will I? I truly do not think so. For one thing, I'm seven years older than Ruthie, which has to account for something. And after riding the rapids of the last few months, relying only on myself, I have developed a sturdy and unemotional backbone when it comes to the inevitable.

Sunday evening, September 12

They brought the babies at ten this morning, just like the nurse said. While Ruthie cried into her daughter's blanket, I got a first look at my son. I wasn't prepared. After all my tough talk, I wasn't prepared. This is our son, William's and mine, and it breaks my heart to give him up. William said he wanted a son one day. Well, here he is. A stamped-out little miniature it seems to me, right down to the chin dimple.

I built up a wall of detachment, just held him on my lap as he slept. I let him sleep and fell into a doze myself, which kept me from climbing that wall. Listening to Ruthie fall apart in the next bed, I wondered if it would be me in a couple days. I started to worry. She had reached the end of the separation process they warned about. I had just begun.

Ruthie left at noon and I was alone, leaning against a mound of pillows when they served me lunch. A nurse brought the baby in again at two. I held him on my chest this time. He rooted at my neck, searching, wanting. He knew me! I decided to try nursing him. They said it might not go so well the first time, but no. Eager and demanding, he fed, draining me of the wall and all my determination. His eyebrows were drawn together in concentration, tiny fist pressed against my breast as though making certain his amazing discovery didn't escape. Then, satiated and satisfied, he slept. For the first time in my life, I know what real love is. I thought I loved William, but this is something else and I'll never be the same again.

Like every other mother in the world, I unwrapped his blanket. He was so tiny! Seeing his toes made me laugh. He's a perfect little cherub, worth every bit of the anguish from the last few months. To adequately describe him I'd need better words—one more perfect than perfect, finer than fine. What am I supposed to do now? If only William could see him. He'd want him, want us, I feel sure.

Wednesday, September 15

Adoption papers keep appearing with insistent appeals to sign. The usual stay after delivery for normal women is two weeks. For us from the Home, three days. I'm spending my time in turmoil, joyous one minute and desperate the next.

Joyous, believing I can keep our son and go home with confidence that William will come around. One look at this boy would do it, and I could make it happen with a trip to Camp Forrest. We can get married there with nobody the wiser. Oh, I feel wonderful at the thought! Part of me wants to go directly to Camp Forrest. Seems risky, though, and I'm running out of cash. Better to go home and try from there. It means telling another lie, that William and I have been married for months and kept it a secret, fearing the wrath of the Judge.

But then, despair. William's reaction is as unsure as the weather. The risk of taking the baby home without any assurance, the Judge's anger and certain rejection if it doesn't work out. He might end up kicking me and my son right out of the house.

But why go back to the Judge? My sister would welcome us, surely, while I work things out. Her own good William has gone off to war so it's just her and Grace. Evelyn will be okay once she gets over her annoyance that I never confessed any of this. And, won't Gracie be excited about her new little cousin! She just turned nine, shaken to the bone about her father going to war. Can't quite imagine how that must feel. It would be a liberation if the Judge ever left.

This is how it has been day and night, joy to despair and back again. I've waited until the last moment to decide. The truth is, I just can't give him up. Instead of signing adoption papers, I'm giving him his name: William Avery Dollarhide, Jr, after his father.

Saturday, September 18

I barely remember how Thursday began, except that I was happy as I dressed him in the little yellow layette. On the short taxi ride to the station, my mind was filled with pleasant thoughts, all burdens lifted. I'd made my choice.

The trip back east was certainly better than the trip west, which seemed a hundred years ago. It was dusty on the train and a bit noisy, but little Avery seemed content, his contentment mirrored in me. In the easy company of a newborn who did nothing but sleep, I assessed my situation as I saw it then. Basically, I was forcing William's hand. What choice would he have? Agree to go along and marry me, or refuse and look like a louse. My reputation would be ruined but so would his. And, I still had the secret. For our son's sake, I'd remind him if necessary, but only if forced. I prayed it wouldn't come to that because I hated to begin our marriage with a threat.

I decided it would be best to call Evelyn in Norton, and not just show up at the door. At one point, while I practiced what to say to her, Avery opened his eyes and stared at me. He seemed to understand and I think he even smiled. "Everything will be fine, my little cherub, you'll see," I said, riding on a mountain of hope as large as the locomotive out front.

I thought my life had already taken its sharpest turns, that I'd already had all my shocks. But life laughed at me and proved me wrong at the Norton Train Station. I got another jolt there, another punch in the stomach, and I couldn't run home and hide in my room. This time, it was a headline and a photograph on the newsstand, and they took the fight right out of me.

Heiress to Capshaw Foundry Empire Marries Local Businessman

The photograph said it all—my smiling, uniformed William, his arm around Trixie Capshaw dressed in a wedding gown and veil.

Lt. William Dollarhide, on leave from Camp Forrest Tennessee, married Trixie Lynn Capshaw, daughter of Foundry Tycoon Howard Capshaw, Thursday evening after a hurried war-time courtship. The couple plan a short honeymoon in Roanoke ....

I escaped to the ladies' washroom. It was the best I could do. In one of the stalls, I threw up in the toilet with Avery propped on my shoulder.

"Are you all right? Anything I can do?" a kind woman asked at the stall door.

"No, I'm fine, better now," I said, telling the biggest lie of my life.

I sat in the stall a long time, unable to think. When thoughts finally came, they were harsh. Can't go home now, can't go home. Rejection from the Judge, shunned by the town. I nestled Avery against my chest at the thought. Bad for me, yes, but worse for him. Never to be accepted as legitimate, whispered looks, speculation about who fathered him. And what would I tell him one day? Make up a story or tell him the truth, a truth he could never claim.

Just a few days ago I wanted a new start for myself. Well, what about Avery, innocent in all this. He's the one deserving of a fresh start. What if William's secret came out? How selfish to throw a defenseless baby into the middle of this mess. He needed an untarnished name.

I read a story once about a baby girl left outside a fire station, and how she got adopted to a good home. I thought it was awful. How could a mother do that, I wondered, so judgmental then. Now, I know. Now I understand how desperate the mother must have been, backed into a corner with no way out. This was better, wasn't it? A station full of people where he'd be immediately found.

In the washroom stall I nursed him, cuddled him. Oddly, I shed no tears, hardening myself to what lay ahead. And I'd have the rest of my life to cry. Back in the waiting area I placed him on a bench and walked around a bit, separating myself.

When they called my train I went to the ticket window and said, nodding, "Sir, I believe that baby has been left unattended." Then, before the man could do anything, I quit the building to board my train, leaving Avery there for strangers to look after. I was doing it for my sweet baby's sake but it sure didn't feel like it.

Within a few hours my breasts were full and uncomfortable. Good. I welcome misery. Let them throb and ache for days, a fitting reminder of what I have done. The Judge was right all along. I'm a fool.

Abandoning Avery will haunt me the rest of my life. How can I be happy? I don't want to be happy.

I'll never be happy again.

Six

Grace Dawson   **June, 1951**

Oh, Aunt Clara's words! I felt her despair and it hurt. That train station account, her last journal entry ever, the way it finished so dark and sudden-like, you could say it was a lot like her life. I found myself of two minds about it, grateful to be alone to collect my thoughts. On one hand I felt so bad about her predicament, yet it seemed such an awful thing to do.

And, William Dollarhide! What a terrible man! I kept thinking Obie would never treat me that way, but had poor Aunt Clara thought the same?

Obie and I had played around in his truck. Just the other night we got carried away down by Morris Creek. When I came to my senses we were still a long way from doing it, but I got a strong feeling of the shifting sands the preacher talks about in church.

Together, we escaped the truck. Obie draped an arm around me and we made it to the edge of the creek, feeling our way in the dark. We didn't say anything, either of us.

Obie picked up a pebble and skimmed it across the water, just by the touch because he couldn't see. We heard it hit once, and again, and then again before it sank.

I pictured my mother finding out what we'd been doing. Or, good gosh, my father! Nobody would approve, except maybe Obie. Now, after reading Aunt Clara's words, I decided we'll never go that far again, not until I take his name.

Later, I showed Obie the journal and watched his face as he read. Several times, he glanced over at me. Finally, he blurted, "I know what you're thinking, but I'm not William Dollarhide. I'd never do that to you."

"I believe you, really I do. But, just so you know, I don't plan to give you the chance." He seemed a bit hurt so I took out the sting with a kiss on the cheek, though I meant every word.

"We should show the journal to Pop," he said, "let him read it for himself."

"Yes, especially this part, 'William trusts me not to tell ... such a horrible secret, though.' Aunt Clara's talking about the killing right there."

"No doubt about it."

"And, look. Did you notice pages are missing? Seems like she just ripped them out."

When we handed the journal to the Chief, he read the entire thing with several long, low whistles, a deep frown appearing early on his face and not going away. "All of this is ... well ... it's shocking. Interesting as it is, though, it's not about the killing. She seems to hint at it but it's not enough."

He flipped through the journal one more time. "Pages are missing here in front. Curious."

"Maybe they were about the killing. That's why she tore them out," I said.

"Sounds plausible. Have you tried to find them?"

"Not yet. I'm afraid she threw them away. Why? Would they help?"

"I doubt it, but I'd find an account of the killing damned interesting. Excuse me, Grace. It's always eaten at me that we didn't take any action against Dollarhide. He was drafted into the Army in the middle of it, then married the Capshaw girl. After the war, his father-in-law named him director of something that hadn't existed before, and he was off and running."

The Chief handed the journal back to me, stuck a finger in his ear and shook it. "Written accounts and a woman's dying declaration aren't worth much in a courtroom. Don't know what you two expected but I can't move forward with this, however much I'd like to. It proves the man's a cad but we already knew that. And it's not against the law to father a child out of wedlock."

It was the same kind of thing he'd said before. Even with Aunt Clara's journal, we hadn't made any progress at all.

The following Saturday, I took the train back to Norton to learn more about the boy. Too, I hoped to find the perfect prom dress in the bigger town. I wasn't especially particular, except it had to be long, it had to be sleeveless, it had to be dreamy, and it had to be pink.

During this trip, the sun shined a spotlight on the show. Rolling hills rushing by, pretty little valleys nestled between mountains, a field of buttercups, another of laurel. A sight to behold on one hand but no grander, really, than out my own bedroom window. Sometimes, the view got cut off by trees hugging the tracks close enough to scrape the train. When we stopped in Pound, my view stayed put a few minutes—cows nosing for grass, farmer hoeing a garden. And in the sudden quiet, a woodpecker went to work on a tree trunk nearby. All of them busy but me.

I wondered about Aunt Clara on the same train years earlier. She must have felt so alone in the world, afraid of tomorrow, nobody to turn to, no way to escape. If the same thing happened to me, who would I turn to? Hard to imagine anything worse.

In Norton, I tackled the shopping first. Now, I'll admit the dress was important but putting it first didn't mean anything. It just worked out that way. On the walk from the station to the taxi stand, the perfect dress, a baby-pink formal, called out to me from a storefront window. I tried it on, paid for it in a quick fifteen minutes, and the lady agreed to hold it behind the counter.

My second visit to the adoption agency went as well as the dress, and a far sight better than my first visit. The difference was Mrs. Weaver. When I walked in, she was watering potted plants with a cheery look on her face, fondling the leaves as though they were her children. I liked her immediately. "Oh yes, I remember the case well. Who could forget? Cutest little boy you ever saw, decked out in a store-bought yellow layette. Dressed too warm for September but most new mothers do that."

I pulled out the journal and read her some passages, the ones showing Aunt Clara's desperation, the guilt and anguish later because of what she'd done.

"Hearing that just breaks my heart. I knew there had to be a good reason," Mrs. Weaver said, fighting back tears. "Have a seat while I find the file."

She disappeared into another room and came back with a folder labeled:

Unidentified—Norton Train Station, September 17, 1943.

"I always hoped this case would be resolved." Treating the folder itself like a baby, she placed it on the desk and opened it. "Look, here's the little layette and blanket. Faded and a bit dingy now, but time has done that. It was obviously expensive. And look at this, a note pinned to his blanket:

I called him Avery, after his father. Tell him I'll always love him.

Doesn't it just break your heart?"

The safety pin had rusted in place. It was Aunt Clara's handwriting, all right—high, tight, and on a slant. So, this was real. I fumbled for a handkerchief with my own teary eyes.

Mrs. Weaver suddenly thought of something to do in the other room, but I think she was just giving me space. She returned a few minutes later with a glass of water and handed it to me. "You okay?"

"I am now, thank you. It was just a shock. Is Mullin the family's name?"

"Why, yes, how do you know?"

"Aunt Clara was a second-grade teacher in Betula. When he walked in her classroom last September, she recognized him."

"Well, isn't that something!"

"She came up here to find out, but she got that other woman, the nasty one, instead of you. Aunt Clara was never happy after the train station, but she really went downhill then."

"Oh, dear. Yes, Myrna can be difficult. I try not to make judgments about the birth mothers. The way I see it, your aunt was in a tough spot and saw no other options, so she left her baby where she knew he'd be quickly found. Such a sad case, really. They're all sad but this one touched me deeper."

Mrs. Weaver set the baby clothes aside and picked up a pen. "Now, I can add this new information and take the file out of Unidentified. Mother: Clara Anne Bond, deceased. Do you know the identity of the father?"

"Uh, really can't say," I said, not wanting to outright lie.

"Can't say, or won't say?"

"Uh ..."

She smiled. "I would like to have it for the file, is all. It will remain confidential."

I quickly changed the subject, afraid to tell her. "Maybe you already know, but Mr. Mullin died last year."

"Yes, it's in the file. And I see that the adopting parents had a keen interest in the real parents, wanted to connect with them for the sake of the boy."

"So, it's okay for me to visit the family?" Tears welled up again from no more doubts. That blond-headed little Henry with the droopy socks was my first cousin.

"Don't see why not. Just let me know how it turns out so I can–"

"I know, so you can update the file."

We both laughed at that and it helped. "Thanks for being so kind. I keep thinking, if you'd been here the day Aunt Clara came, instead of the nasty one ... what's her name?"

"Myrna Lawson."

"If you'd been here instead of Myrna Lawson, Aunt Clara could be visiting the family."

Seven

Before going any further, I need to tell you something about myself. My dad has always called me psychic, even when I was a kid. "You are just like your Grandmother Dawson," he'd say. Impossible to surprise with birthday parties and such. Then, there was the time I draped my arm around his neck and begged him not to go, weeks before he'd even gotten a draft notice.

I sometimes sense trouble—arm hairs standing straight up, galloping pulse, tingling between the eyebrows—and I can't remember a time when these signs lied. I named them the prickly willys back then and it stuck. Chewing gum helps when I get the willys. Gives me a place to target the tension. Over the years I have turned into quite a gum chewer, though mother says it's unladylike and we're not allowed to chew gum in school.

I'm a vivid dreamer and most of the time they don't mean a thing. I often dreamt of dinosaurs as a kid. Did you do that? In my dreams, we had dinosaur season like the hurricane season down south. A dinosaur as big as a mountain would stomp through Betula once a year on its way somewhere and cause a tremendous shake. We'd all throw up our arms in a panic, run to the closet and hide. Just silly little kid dreams, nothing real about them. But, now and then, I get one that feels real as rain. The trick is knowing the difference and that's where the prickly willys come in. I never got the willys after a dinosaur dream.

One more thing, I tend to be superstitious. Grandmother once said, if you step out of the house with your right foot instead of your left, things will more likely go your way. Don't know if it's true but I believe in starting out like that, just in case.

So, here's a question: Can weather influence an outcome? I mean, if it's raining on the day of the big exam or interview for a summer job, is there less chance for success? Mr. Grant says no. I say yes.

It was sunny and seventy the day I met Mrs. Mullin, and the upshot of it bore my theory out. She was coming up the walk with a bag of groceries and I helped her open the door. Not a bad start. But how do you begin a conversation like the one I needed to have. I didn't know, so I just introduced myself, which was her cue to say how sorry she was about my aunt. She offered me a seat on the couch and I took it. Then, she looked at me with pleasant curiosity, wondering why I was there.

"Mrs. Mullin, where is Henry right now?" I asked, figuring it ought to be her choice what to tell him.

"Please, call me Mary. He's playing next door. Why? Is everything all right?"

"Well, I think it's wonderful. Hope you think it's all right. I have information about Henry's birthmother." And then, right or wrong, to her surprised face, I just blurted it out, giving her no more warning than Aunt Clara had given me.

Over lemonade and little cakes we talked for an hour. Actually, it was mostly me talking—Aunt Clara's situation as an unwed mother, followed by years of guilt and regret. "She recognized him, or thought she did, when he walked into her classroom. But she'd seen him a hundred times before in the faces of little boys on the street."

"She did?" Mary dabbed at her cheeks with a faded handkerchief.

"She tried to find out, went back to the agency and asked if it could be him. They wouldn't say. Well, that woman, Myrna Lawson, wouldn't say. So, after more than seven years of pain and guilt, she gave up everything." Mary was openly crying now and part of me felt bad. But it was a good kind of crying, better than believing Henry's mother didn't care. "For what it's worth, he was loved, if only from a distance. Every day, every minute, she thought of him."

"Do you know who the father is?"

There it was again, that question. This was no time for truth telling so I lied and said I didn't. "At least now he'll know his mother's family," I said, trying to move from the lie. "I'm his first cousin and I want to be part of his life, if that's okay."

"Of course, it's okay! It's wonderful!"

"How has it been for you since you lost your husband? Financially, I mean."

"Well, it's rough, I don't mind saying. With no money coming in, I had to get a job and leave Henry with a kind neighbor."

"I inherited everything Aunt Clara owned. There isn't much money but she'd want you to have it."

We decided she would tell Henry in her own way. The sad thing was, however she told him, he'd find his mother and lose her again, all at the same time. It was enough to water your eyes.

>*>*>*<*<*<

With high school classes and term papers over for the summer, Obie and I were free to poke around in the storage room for Donnie Ray Carr's old files.

And we talked to Officer Ernie Reed who'd been fresh to the force back in 1943. "We were both sure something bad happened to Donnie Ray, the Chief and me, because the man wouldn't just vanish into the wind like that. And we figured William Dollarhide had something to do with it."

"Do you remember the day he disappeared?" Obie asked.

"Like it was yesterday. In the morning, Donnie Ray hauled Lenny Bridge in for a drunk-and-disorderly, served papers on Quiggy Jones. Then in the afternoon, well, first he tried to get Dollarhide on the telephone, wanted him to come in and answer some questions about shady contracts at the highway commission. When that didn't work, he went out looking for Dollarhide, hoped to run into him unexpected-like, try to rattle him. It wasn't only about shady contracts, though. Donnie Ray was sweet on that girl."

"Which girl?" I asked.

"That juicy young thing Dollarhide was seeing."

"You mean, Aunt Clara?"

"Oh, hell, I guess it was."

"Donnie Ray was sweet on Aunt Clara?"

"Yeah, buddy, but it didn't do him any good. She only had eyes for Dollarhide and it really pissed Donnie Ray off. He thought she deserved better, kept hoping Judge Bond would put a stop to it."

I sat there stunned and hardly listened, tripping over the image of my old-maid aunt as a "juicy young thing."

"Sorry, Grace, I forgot," Ernie said. "Hard to match that girl up with ..."

"It's okay, having a hard time with it myself." But the idea pleased me.

Ernie took the lid off a box labeled D.R. Carr and pulled out an accordion folder. "Here's what you want, everything Donnie Ray had on William Dollarhide. We went through it all at the time, but it didn't buy us nothing."

Obie carried the folder to an empty desk, pulled out all the papers and studied the one on top.

"Hmm, can you read his writing?" I asked. "He must have flunked penmanship."

"All good cops have crummy handwriting. They do not have the time or the patience to be neat. Look what it says here. 'Suspected Charges: Using undue influence in granting awards for local road contracts, receiving kickbacks.' Donnie Ray was going after Dollarhide for graft and corruption. Pop approved it. See his signature?"

Obie set that paper aside and studied the one under it. "He took these notes in an interview with Lynwood Brown over in Grundy. Maybe we should go talk to Lynwood. We can at least do that much."

"Will it do us any good?"

"I dunno. Maybe he'll have more to say about Dollarhide now. Even a hint of shady deals in the newspaper could hurt him in the next election."

"Okay, I like the sound of that."

But a day or two later, on the drive to Grundy, graft and corruption seemed trivial compared to shoving a cop to his death.

We found Lynwood Brown at a construction site trailer. In muddy boots and coveralls, he was eager to share what he knew, plus a few other things he merely assumed. "Some said I had an axe to grind and I reckon it's true enough. When somebody messes with food on the table, well, you can't just let it slide. I was bidding for jobs and got a few. It all felt fair. Then, William Dollarhide came along and … no more jobs. Wasn't just me. Andy Walker's business dried up, too. Most the jobs went to the Parker brothers while the rest of us were scratching our heads. Gotta admit, though, I had my chance."

"What do you mean?" Obie asked.

"We were having a beer at the pub, me and Dollarhide, and he said plain as day, 'One favor for another. That's how it works.' I must have looked at him funny because he added, 'It's all a game, my friend. I can get you the jobs if you wanna play.' Now, that was an invitation. He was looking for more than just a drink across the bar and I didn't bite. Wasn't too smart of him to speak so plain."

"Did you tell Donnie Ray Carr?"

"Sure, I did. But then he disappeared and, well, you know the rest."

"What do you think happened to him?"

"Dollarhide got rid of him, since you asked."

"A lot of folks believe that. No proof, though," Obie said, staring at me.

"Yeah, even the other charges were difficult to prove. The ones who were playing were not gonna talk, slogging around in illegal territory, bribery territory, themselves. When they saw the law coming after Dollarhide they ran for cover. Interesting thing was, once he married into the Capshaw's and moved on, I started getting jobs again, me and Andy. The Parkers eventually went out of business. We enjoyed that."

Lynwood lit his pipe and pointed it at us. "Now, I heard this third hand, but Dollarhide apparently sold Army supplies by the case during the war and made himself a boatload of extra cash on the black market for rationed goods."

"Jesus, that's low," Obie said.

"Yeah, if the man got hit by a freight train I'd be okay. He's at the statehouse, now, bigger fish in the bigger pond. But he's a blowfish, poison to whatever body of water he's in. I'm getting wind of the same kind of shenanigans going on in Richmond. A construction contract, a big one, just went out for a dam near Roanoke. Buddy of mine says it don't feel right and I'd bet my Sunday socks it isn't."

Lynwood rubbed a thumb and finger together to imply a money deal. "Yeah, Dollarhide's living high on the hog with the state boys now. Okay by me. At least he's not polluting our little pond anymore. He's left enemies behind, though, that's for sure. And there's one more thing." Lynwood lifted an eyebrow and grinned. "Rumor has it there's a girlfriend in Richmond. He spends a lot of time up there so it would be easy for him to mess around on the side. Taking a chance, seems to me. Could upset his whole damn applecart. Howard Capshaw is a powerful man, upstate as well as here. If he gets wind that the son-in-law is cheating on his little Trixie, and you know he eventually will, things could turn ugly. Okay by me. There's a few of us here who'd enjoy watching. Some might even like to help it along."

I wanted so much to tell Lynwood about Aunt Clara, see his reaction, but I knew better than to spill it on a whim. Once words are said, they are out there for good.

Eight

For me, the summer of 1951 meant working in my dad's law office in town, right down the street from the police station. Obie took care of the family garden and continued to tend the apple orchard, which earned him the right to hang around the station the rest of the time. No official police work, his father was quick to add. Just follow orders, which mostly meant keeping up the Wanted board, organizing files, and the evidence shelves. Once, he was permitted to man the telephones for an entire morning while Ernie was gone and the Chief went to a meeting in Wise, the county seat.

Turned out, a surprising thing happened and I think it was fate. Mr. Mason from the hardware store called to report his daughter missing, hadn't seen her in two days. There was worry in his voice, Obie said.

My eyebrows went up when I heard. Nettie Mason was in our class at school and we'd all seen her with a rough and muscled logging-camp worker named Roy, who didn't live around here. That's cause enough for a father to worry, seems to me. I know we aren't supposed to make snap judgments about people but it's a tough-looking bunch at that camp. Workers come from all around and they bunk out there in cabins. Any girl messing with one of them is just asking for trouble, is all I'm saying.

Although, Nettie hadn't been missing for as long as two days. The day before, I had seen her walking down Berkey Road. When I tooted my horn and asked if she wanted a lift, she merely shook her head and kept on going. She attempted to hide her face with her hair, but I could see her eyes were red and puffy from crying. I told Obie.

"Was she walking toward town or away from town?"

"Away."

"Maybe she was heading to the logging camp."

"No, she'd already passed the road to the camp."

"Hmm, wonder where she was headed. Nothing out that way but the river and tarpaper shacks down a holler." Obie glanced at the clock on the wall. "I'd like to go talk to this guy, Roy, see what he has to say."

"Your father wouldn't like it."

"Yeah, he'd say I'm not authorized to get involved. Matter of fact, knowing him, he might even refuse to let me work here anymore."

An hour or so later, Ernie Reed showed up and Obie filled him in. Ernie went straight out to the camp himself, but soon came back. According to the log foreman, Roy left camp late one night and took all his gear with him. Didn't sound good.

Obie decided it would not be getting too involved to take a ride down Berkey Road with the hound dogs, and I decided to go with him. We went to Mr. Mason's place first to borrow something of Nettie's. He gave us a scarf. Then, Obie swung home to get Buster and Blue.

The dogs were brown as pennies, both of them. Looked alike enough to be brothers but they were actually father and son. Eager and sneezing with excitement, they piled into the back of the truck. Riding in a truck must be the best thing in the world to dogs. As Obie sped down Berkey Road, ball-hooting it for their benefit, they faced into the wind on shaky legs, fur flattened, eyes half closed and slanted back, giving Obie's darlings a slightly oriental look. On bumps in the road they wobbled and nearly fell twice. Pure bliss.

"Have they ever tracked a person before?" I asked.

"No, this'll be a first, but I don't expect it to be much different." Obie went a mile or so past the entrance to the logging camp, let the dogs out, gave them a sniff of Nettie's scarf and said, "Find her, boys! Find!" They took off further down Berkey, noses to the road, howling. Obie jumped back into the truck and we followed. A mile later, at the mouth of Jobe's Holler, the hounds paused long enough to give the ground a good sniff. Then they turned to Obie and howled louder, as if making sure he took notice. He yelled, "Stay, boys! Stay!"

Around here we have the extremes when it comes to roads, from freshly paved county roads to crude dirt hollers that can really wrack up a truck. I'd never been down Jobe's Holler but Obie had. He said it was rough going, involved even crossing a creek filled with rocks, some near the size of his mother's henhouse. He parked the truck and we got out. The dogs sat on their haunches while Obie fit them with harnesses and twenty-foot leads. They didn't like it one little bit, quivering madly until Obie released them again with, "Find her!"

They sniffed a few mailboxes and then took off down the holler. I could barely keep up. At the creek, the dogs spent a few confused seconds sniffing back and forth along the edge. Then they splashed across it and picked up the scent again.

Houses paired with outhouses appeared in breaks of the trees. Many in Betula have indoor plumbing but not on Jobe's Holler, or any holler for that matter. We have indoor plumbing, Mother and I, thanks to Dad. He had it put in four years ago. And, what did my mother do? She thanked him without even a smile, then danced with joy when he wasn't around. A few months later she had the outhouse bulldozed so she wouldn't have to look at it.

Anyway, the houses on Jobe's Holler did not seem sturdy enough to live in, but I guess they were. A woman was beating dust out of a rug with a broom, her two little girls on their knees making mud pies near a well pump. Further along, another woman sat on a porch with one child on her lap and three more at her feet. Actually, most houses had porches with people sitting on them. If they weren't already there, the noise of the hounds brought them out. What we were doing, though, held no particular fascination for these people since hunting with hounds was almost an everyday thing.

But their dogs? They all joined the howling and some tried to join the hunt, running in circles around Buster and Blue until the owners called them back or Obie chased them away. It went on like that for maybe a half mile more. I could soon smell the river and the air felt damper.

In the distance, we saw a girl who looked like Nettie standing on the porch of a ramshackle house. Too far away to be sure at first, but then the dogs strained harder at their leads, and we knew. For a moment, it looked like they might drag Obie down on his face, trying to get at her.

Even before we set foot in the yard, Nettie opened the screen door and bolted into the house. Don't know if it was the dogs that scared her, or the sight of us. The dogs sure scared a rooster away from scratching up a meal in the dirt.

Obie yelled, "Stay, boys!" and those poor dogs stopped, glued to the ground and whining. He'd ruined all their fun only a few yards from the prize. To make up for it he rubbed their heads, crooned "good dogs, good dogs" and gave them bacon from breakfast.

He stayed there with them while I went on. Probably just as well. The porch looked ready to collapse if we all stood on it at once. The whole house seemed tilted to the right. I knocked three times, called her name, and went in when she didn't answer. She was sitting white faced on a broken-down couch, knees to her chin, barefoot.

I took a seat across from her on a rickety wood chair. Her socks were hanging on the back of it, dry and stiff, probably from a wade in the creek. I kicked off my shoes, peeled away my wet socks and draped them next to hers.

"Better wring 'em out first or they'll never dry," she said. "Maybe put 'em on the porch in the sun. Shoes, too."

"Good idea," I said, and then went and did it. Back in the chair I gave her a chance to say more. After a minute or two of silence, I said, "Your father is worried."

She still didn't say anything, just wrapped hair around her finger like I do, and studied the floor.

"Smells like cats in here," I said.

"Yeah, the old widow woman took in strays. She died last month."

"Did you know her?"

"No, but Roy did. After she died we met here a few times, him and me."

I could not imagine mixing this place with romance. "How did you stand the smell?"

"Got used to it, I reckon. We could sit on the back porch if you want." She unfolded herself from the couch, opened the screen door for me and let it slam behind her. It was better outside, and we had a view of the river.

"What are you doing out here? Planning to meet Roy?" I wondered if she knew he left town.

"I'm not seeing him no more." From the pain on her face she looked ready to sob. "And jumping in there was my only plan." She nodded at the river.

"You mean ... to drown yourself? Gosh, Nettie, but why?"

She confessed it all to me then. Roy got her pregnant. She had let herself get taken in by promises of travel and a paper ring. I didn't know what to say, reminded of Aunt Clara. Had she, too, wanted to die? We sat for a while just watching the river.

"Weren't you afraid out here last night, all alone?" I asked.

"Nah, the toad frogs made a racket at first, and then it rained. The sound of it hitting the tin roof was peaceful, put me in mind of home. I come onto a raccoon in the outhouse this morning, though. It liketa scared the bejesus outta me." She gave me a weak smile.

I smiled back. After a pause I said, "Your father's really worried. He's been thinking the worst."

"Don't know what he thinks is the worst, but this is the worst in my book. Funny thing. It don't hurt so much any-more, Roy walkin' out on me. Shoot, my ideas about him have already sunk to bottom." Nettie combed her hair back with her fingers and scratched her arm. "But I was such a sucker. Roy made a dozen promises and I swallowed them whole. Now, my life ain't worth an Indian-head cent, not after what I let him do to me. And, here, I done spent all my money on him, money I saved all year."

Out of sympathy, I patted her arm. "Money's one thing, Nettie, your life's another. I sure hope you've given up on the river idea."

"Yeah, I already tried once, jumped slap-right into it and straight down. But I swim strong and the current's weak. See how slow it's running?" She nodded at the river again. "It let me change my mind instead of taking me."

"Wasn't your time, then. Are you ready to go home?"

"That's the part I just can't stand. I'm too ashamed, and it'll kill my daddy." Her eyes got shiny with tears. "He don't know nothing about this yet and he'll be so disappointed. On top of that, we'll both be disgraced."

"You aren't giving him enough credit, Nettie. Mostly, he'll be relieved you're okay."

She glared at me with open doubt.

"I said, mostly. Sure, he'll be disappointed at first but he'd rather have you home like this than not at all."

"Pretty thoughts, but I still can't disgrace him."

"What are you gonna do, then? You can't stay out here. Aren't you hungry?"

"Reckon so. All I had since yesterday was cornpone."

I told her about the Salvation Army Home in Louisville, how the train out of Norton goes right there, and I knew somebody once who was in the same fix and things turned out okay. I know, I know. That part was a lie. But what else could I say? After all, she'd been plotting suicide out there. I mean, boy oh boy, something was wrong when getting pregnant without a wedding was right up there with dying.

We talked more about Louisville—how nobody in town needed to know, she could get the telephone number for the Salvation Army Home from the operator and then just call them up long distance. Laying out the steps seemed to help. At least now she had a third choice, something other than suicide or disgrace.

"Let's go. You must be starved," I said, appealing to her stomach. By the time we got her home, she had plucked up the courage to face her father and make the call to Louisville. She was still riding the fence about the adoption idea. Part of me wanted to tell her about Aunt Clara, but of course I could not.

Obie and I felt good about the entire thing, a little taste of how it will be someday, working together. We were just disappointed we couldn't blame this one on Dollarhide.

The Chief complained that we should not have gone looking for Nettie, but I think he was secretly pleased. We had settled the situation in an afternoon and it never even made the newspaper. He told Obie, "You showed restraint by not barging into that logging camp. Part of being a good cop is knowing your limitations, so I'm proud of you there. But," He looked at his son hard and pointed a finger, "none of it changes the fact that you're going to college." Case closed.

Nine

Unlike Obie, I want to go to college, need to go if I'm to become a lawyer. Mother wants me to do better than she did so she supports my college plans, especially since Dad promised to pay for it. She says, before the war, all a woman could do in this town was get married, dress hair or teach.

During the war she got herself a job at the cement factory and then lost it again when the men came home. Now, she works in the office at the Piggly Wiggly three afternoons a week. She claims it's merely to get out of the house, but I suspect it's just as much about the fifteen percent she saves on groceries, being an employee.

There isn't a college within a hundred miles so I have to go away, but I'd remain right here in Betula if I could. These mountains are my home.

I can guess what you're thinking. What do I know of the world, what have I seen to already be so content to stay in the same spot. It's true that I have never been to an ocean or desert, or anywhere beyond these hills. I've seen pictures of palm trees, and of faraway places I hope to visit one day. Yet, without going anywhere I often stumble upon a stupendous view I hadn't seen before. And when I witness a fiery sunset against the green of the farthest mountain, or the peaceful fog of a morning before it gets burned off ... well, I say there's nothing wrong with here.

Most of my friends feel different. They can't wait to be gone. And, shortly after the Nettie incident, when Obie's cousin Lucy came from Brooklyn to stay two weeks, she certainly wasn't impressed with my hometown.

Frankly, I didn't like her much, either. According to Lucy, we're all just wasting away out here, cut off from culture and the modern age in these piney back woods. She told us about seeing *Brigadoon* on Broadway and I acted impressed like she wanted me to, though it didn't mean a thing. She seemed a bit stuck up, and too stylish for my taste. I know, I know. You think I'm just jealous, but listen. She said people here have lazy eyes, move too slow and talk with a twang. Do we? She said we use double negatives. I don't do that because Mother wouldn't let me, but okay, yeah, some people down here do.

If Lucy thought so little of us, why didn't she just stay home? My father would probably find her remarks insulting. We're not cut off from the modern age. We see it *all* down here. The foundry people, and the coal people, too, drive automobiles a mile long that come in every color, able to cool down the inside air, even on the hottest day. Dollarhide cruises around town in a white Cadillac with red upholstery, best looking car I ever saw.

Other amazing modernities come to us on the pages of magazines. Why, just last week there was a washing machine for dishes, the most bewitching idea yet. If I piled dishes into our washing machine and turned it on, they'd rattle around and bang against each other so much that every single one would come out broken.

Getting back to Lucy, she bragged about living on Foster Avenue where a person can find chop suey and pizza pie, all manner of food, day or night. We took her to Jerky's, the best we have to offer for dining out. It's famous. I mean, people travel miles for a Jerky's chili hot dog. We ordered her one. She took a cautious bite and didn't say a word.

"Can you guess what's in the chili?" I asked with a little grin, certain she'd be stumped like the rest of us by the handed-down secret recipe.

"Cumin," she said, without a pause. Cumin? I had never heard of cumin. None of us had. She called it "a surprising find in this hillbilly cuisine," which meant she approved of it, I guess.

"Have you ever seen the Empire State Building?" I asked her.

"Of course! More than that, I've been up in it."

"Gosh, what was it like?"

"You see forever up there. You can see the entire world."

Now, that I wouldn't mind. Although, can't we see just as far from up on the break?

Sometime during her second week, Lucy stopped talking of home long enough to notice Mrs. Sayer's cooking. When the peaches, corn and tomatoes started coming in, and Lucy got to sample fried chicken from a hen that had run around the barnyard in the morning and gotten its head lopped off that very afternoon, she finally found something to like about Betula. She marveled at how delicious it all was, seemed surprised that such good food had come from sun, seeds and dirt.

I don't want to be cruel, but I think she'd put on a few pounds when she took the train home.

By the time Lucy went back to Brooklyn, those missing journal pages were definitely eating at me. And Obie, too, wouldn't leave the subject alone. We both felt sure that Aunt Clara had written about what happened at the break, thought better of it and ripped the pages out.

But we differed in our hopes for finding them. He was certain she hid them somewhere. I was certain she destroyed them. Doesn't that make the most sense? Why else would she have ripped them out. But then the Chief got involved and gave us a direct order to search, so my opinion didn't matter.

After the birth certificate, only a few parts of the house were left to explore. The dreaded cellar, for one, but Aunt Clara had always avoided the cellar. She wouldn't have put the missing pages down there.

We considered the parlor again and looked where we had already looked, examined the books on the shelves and the stack of stuff that came out of them. Obie lifted the chair cushions, found two pencils with the points broken off, and one dead mouse.

We upturned all the vases. A key fell out of one of them.

"Wonder what it fits?" I asked.

"Dunno, but hang onto it."

"Something else in here, too, Obie. Won't come out, though."

"Lemme see." He shined his flashlight down the neck of it, then stuck long fingers in and wiggled them. "Feels like papers, maybe a magazine or some kind of report."

"Could be the missing pages, then."

"It could be, certainly could be." He blew into it making a sound.

"Can you get them out?"

He shook the vase, banged on the bottom, attempted to grab whatever it was with the tips of his fingers. "Somebody forced it down the neck of this thing and it's not coming out. We'll need to break it."

"Okay, go ahead. It's the ugliest vase I ever saw, and there's another one just like it. Besides, I got a feeling."

He stared at me. "Have you got a hammer?"

I went to the utility room off the kitchen, found one in a drawer and brought it to him.

He tapped gently.

"Harder."

With that, he whacked it a good one and the bottom fell out in pieces on the floor. He reached in and grabbed a tube of papers held in a tight roll with rubber bands. We looked at each other with grins. Easy to see it was a piece of the journal or something else Aunt Clara had written. The pages were heavy with her spidery scrawl. Obie removed the bands and stretched the pages flat. But before we got anywhere reading them, I heard Mother's voice calling my name.

"Get rid of them," I whispered, hurrying to meet her at the door. "Mother, what are you doing here?"

"I just dropped by," she said with suspicion, taking in the broken vase, our hurried movements, Obie's guilty look and my fake smile. "I do not approve of the two of you spending time here alone."

"We're not spending time, exactly. We're going through things, looking for more of Aunt Clara's writings, like you suggested." A little buttering up never hurt. I wasn't prepared to show her what we found, not until I read the pages myself. With her, it's best to take one cautious step at a time.

She hung around awhile, wandered into the Judge's library, climbed the stairs to her old bedroom and came down a few minutes later carrying a lamp. "Want this for the desk in your room, Gracie?"

"Sure. It'll be nice to have more light," I said, meaning it. I walked her to the door and kissed her on the cheek, trying to hide that I wanted her gone. While I stood in the doorway, she seemed to take forever situating herself and the lamp on the front seat of the car, and another forever to start it and be on her way. Finally, it was safe to close the door and hurry back to Obie. I expected to find him already reading. "Where are they?" I asked.

He pointed to the other vase and rolled his eyes. In the excitement, he'd shoved the pages down the narrow neck of *that* vase, which we then had to break.

Ten

Journal of Clara Bond, 1943

Monday, March 22

Nobody knows the predicament I'm in. Not even William, and he's in it with me. No point telling him until I'm certain, and I'm just not certain yet. About this sort of thing I'm not completely ignorant. I remember how it was with Evelyn. Just like with me, her period was late when it had always been regular as sunrise. Just like with me, morning queasiness soon began and she feared the truth right then, but refused to believe. At least she had a husband when it happened to her. Not like with me.

This is serious—an unmarried schoolteacher, daughter of a judge. Why did I let myself get into such a mess? What I need now is a doctor to say for sure, but it can't be one in town.

Wednesday, March 31

This morning I feigned illness, got a substitute to take my place in class, and went to see a doctor in Jenkins, Kentucky.

On the rainy drive over there I told myself I was wrong, that it was commonplace for women to have false alarms. This was merely a well-timed warning to stop taking chances, no more lovemaking until after we married.

But, I knew the truth on the return trip home. As the sun dipped low the temperature dropped, turning the mountain roads icy. I did not even care. Somehow, by comparison, the thought of careening to my death didn't feel like much of a threat.

Then I remembered something else about Evelyn. Just like with me, she did not want the baby. She didn't want it even married to the best of men. But, she soon got over it and now they have sweet little Gracie everyone adores.

This thought cheered me immensely. It could still work out just as well for me, even if things didn't happen in the right order. When I tell William, he'll be happy about it and everything will be fine. We'll need to elope in a hurry. No bridal shower or wedding dress, no invitations, no dancing to Glenn Miller or rice thrown as we depart. But we can still have a honeymoon. And I bet Evelyn will give me a shower anyway, when we return. I feel so much better. It is not unreasonable to expect I'll be a married woman soon. Nothing to do now but tell William.

Monday, April 26

Easter Sunday came and went yesterday. William still doesn't know. It isn't that I haven't tried. Something always stops me—not enough privacy, not enough time. Last Friday, I was waiting for William to come out of the bank when Donnie Ray pulled over to the curb on his motorcycle. He often turns up when I'm in town. He obviously likes me and I think it's sweet. Though, if he knew about my present condition he would change his mind. He asked me to the Chamber of Commerce dance.

"Thanks, but you know I'm seeing William. If I go to the dance, it'll be with him."

"Why are you seeing a man like that?"

"It's clear you don't like him. What is it with you two? He doesn't like you either, and he'll be coming out of the bank any minute."

He ignored my hint to leave. "You seem … mismatched. And, yes, I don't like him."

"You and the Judge. He doesn't like William, either."

"Is that why you're seeing Dollarhide, to get back at your father?"

"Great heavens! Does everything have to be about the Judge?" I turned away and stomped into the drug store leaving Donnie Ray with his mouth open. It wasn't true. I'd made my own choice. I love William, I'm having his child, soon I'll be his bride. It has nothing to do with the Judge.

Frankly, I don't understand why the Judge doesn't like William—engineering degree from VPI, decent job with the Highway Commission at the age of twenty-four, a spot on the state board easily in his future. Most fathers would consider him a catch.

Truthfully, William has never actually proposed marriage, but he's hinted at it more than once. I'm the Judge's daughter, from the highest stock, pillar of the town, and so forth. He talks of wanting a son, and isn't it always part of the same conversation? How else is he to have a son from this good stock except by marrying me. Odd that my father, the thorn of my childhood, is probably my strongest asset. Well, if my pedigree helps me win him, I guess it will make that miserable part of my childhood worthwhile.

When William came out of the bank he was obviously annoyed. He'd seen Donnie Ray talking to me. I could not tell him about the baby while he was angry, so I labeled the opportunity spoiled. Just an excuse, really. Fact is, I'm afraid, my earlier faith was eroded by the delay.

But, it looks like I'll get my big chance tomorrow. William suggested we picnic at the break. I'll pack a lunch, arrange my hair loose around my shoulders the way he likes it, put on his favorite dress. School's out for Easter break, it's spring on the calendar and feels like it. Why, in just a few more days I could actually be Mrs. William Dollarhide!

Tuesday night, April 27

I can't believe it was just earlier today that William came to get me and we headed to the break. Despite my predicament I had high hopes, but the situation is worse now and so much more complicated.

On the way out of town, William spotted Donnie Ray Carr behind us on his motorcycle. "Damn it all to hell, I wish that jackass would leave me alone!" William has always assumed Donnie Ray was following him and not me. He pulled into a gasoline station to get off the road. Donnie Ray kept going.

We had not been up on the break in several months. The trees were in bud, breeze warm, springtime sun as yellow as the flowers in my dress. We spread out a blanket on our usual spot, thirty or so feet from the edge. I did not like being any closer. I set out barbecued pork and apple pie, two of his favorites. Engaging all the weapons from my female arsenal. Seems pathetic now.

While we ate lunch, William started talking about Howard Capshaw, owner of the foundry. He's been doing that a lot lately, talking about the Capshaws and their mansion outside town. They have a daughter near my age but I've never met her. She goes to a private school somewhere.

William finished a pork sandwich and wiped his mouth on a napkin. "I'm supposed to leave for Camp Forrest in a few weeks. But even so, it might not be too late. A job with Capshaw could still buy me an exemption with all those military contracts he's got ..."

I could barely eat, barely think, while he rambled on. I usually listen to every word, share his interest in the future, but it was hard at that moment to make myself care. I waited until he finished talking, until after the pie. Then I told him. Just like that, I told him. I tried to prepare him, gently ease into it, lessen the shock. It didn't work. The moment he realized where I was headed—the look in his eyes, I'll never forget. Like a wild animal, caged.

"This is a fine fix! Your timing stinks, you know that?"

"My timing! What about your timing? You're the one who got me this way."

"What do you expect me to do about it?"

Fear gripped me. It was not going like I imagined. "Isn't it obvious? I expect we'll get married. What else can we do?"

"Damn it, Clara, this is awful! Messes up all my plans."

"What do you mean?"

He glared at me.

"Isn't marriage in your plans?"

"Now, wait a minute. The subject of marriage never came up. I never really asked."

"You said you wanted a son someday, to teach him how to hunt and throw a baseball. You said I'm from good stock. What was all that, if not about marriage?" I dissolved into tears. Didn't intend to, but they just came out. "Don't you love me?" Such a meek, pitiful question.

"Sure I do, but …"

"You said you loved me, many times you said it. Didn't you mean it?"

"Of course, I meant it, insofar as …"

I suppose we were too engrossed to hear Donnie Ray's motorcycle. By the time the sound registered he was up there with us. He parked and dismounted. It silenced us both. As he closed the gap, no doubt taking in my tear-stained face and William's angry one, I wondered how much he'd heard. From the look on his face he'd heard plenty.

William threw darts with his eyes. "What the hell do you want, Carr? This is a private party. You show up everywhere, every time I turn around."

"I'm here on account of you, Dollarhide, to issue a formal summons, signed by Chief Sayer. He wants you to come in for questioning."

"Questioning about what?"

"Possible malfeasance."

"That's ridiculous."

"But more on my mind now is what's going on here." He turned to me. "Clara, is everything okay? You look upset."

William got up off the ground and moved toward Donnie Ray. "That's none of your damn business, Carr. Just issue the summons and get out of here."

"I'm talking to Clara now, and it's very much my business if she's upset."

I didn't answer, too busy wondering what William could have done to interest the Chief of Police. They exchanged more words I didn't hear. When I came out of my stupor, William was angrier than I'd ever seen him, new anger piled on the anger I caused.

He knew better than to get physical with the law, and he never would have done it except for his mood. But he shoved Donnie Ray. He shoved him! It was so unexpected that the policeman lost his footing and stumbled enough to lose his hat. He recovered quickly but William shoved him again! Donnie Ray, more prepared this time, grabbed William's arm and twisted it.

"Stop it you two, stop it!" I yelled, jumping to my feet.

Neither listened. Donnie Ray had special training but William was bigger with training of his own. The two shoved and tripped and slugged each other with such force that all I could do was get out of the way. They went on for what seemed like hours, moving as one, getting further from me, closer to the break.

I cried out again in panic, this time to warn, fearing they would both go over the edge. They were dangerously close! I ran at them, my heart in my throat!

All at once, William shoved with such force that Donnie Ray stumbled back, and back, and back, and ... over! He made such a terrible sound! I will never forget that terrible sound. I stood there gaping into an empty space, stunned. Frantic then, I feared William might fall, too. But he backed out of danger and dropped to his knees, chest heaving.

"We have to get help!" I ran to him, jerked his arm and screamed the same thing again.

"Help? There's no help for this!" He waved an exhausted arm at the edge, barely getting out the words.

"But, we can't just—"

"Nothing we can do! Don't you see that?" He grabbed my hand. "Gather up the blanket and put everything in the car. Go on, do it! We need to leave."

He gripped the motorcycle by the handlebars and seat, began pushing it toward the break.

"What are you doing?"

"Pull yourself together, Clara! Throw all the stuff in the car. We can't leave anything behind."

The bike had been a good twenty feet from the edge, but he pushed it, deliberately pushed it until it, too, went the way of the policeman. Here one second, gone the next!

Escaping down the mountain, neither of us spoke, silence thick, anxious breathing the only sound. He drove straight to an empty church and parked behind it. We sat there trying to recover. "We should go to the police and tell them," I said. "We need to do it now."

"Please, calm down and think, Clara. You know we can't do that. We can't tell anybody."

"William, you just killed a policeman. You must tell."

"I didn't kill him. It was an accident. And what good will telling do? He is gone. They will never find him, never." He pulled me to him and gave me a soft kiss. "Listen, sweetheart, we'll get married like you want, and you'll have the kid and everything will be okay, just like you want. You take care of me and I'll take care of you. All right? You don't want your husband, the father of your child, to live with this hanging over him, do you?"

"No," I said meekly, resting safely in his arms. And then I promised to never tell. I'd take his guilty secret to my grave.

He took me home and I went straight to my room, grateful for the few days to recover before going back to school. Had I witnessed a crime or an accident? An accident, William said. But in an absurd attempt to change the outcome, and almost involuntarily, I keep replaying those final seconds in slow motion—the last fatal push from William, then Donnie Ray stumbling back and back and over the edge. That push seemed deliberate.

I must admit, whether crime or accident, it comes second to me now. The truth is, I have my own problem. The truth is, I'll be showing soon and William will leave for Tennessee. He promised to make everything right. I want to believe him. I want to forget what happened. Nothing we can do about it anyway. William is right about that. Donnie Ray is gone forever, with no trace except in my memory.

Wednesday, April 28

I got no sleep at all last night, tormented by that terrible sound Donnie Ray made as he fell. At one point, I burst into hysterical laughter, which then turned to tears in a violent swerve.

This morning, it's sunny outside but a dark day for me. The reality of yesterday is hitting me in the face. Wadded up in that picnic blanket, I found tangible, undeniable, heartbreaking evidence of the incident I want to forget: Donnie Ray Carr's hat.

Eleven

My mother didn't want me. I got stuck on that part, read it over and over, as Obie moved on.

"Holy cow! She walked away with the hat!" he crowed. "This is amazing! It could change everything! Wait 'til Pop reads this!" He glanced at me. "What are you doing? You're not reading."

"My mother didn't want me."

"What?"

"It's right here in black and white. She didn't want me."

"I'll be damned, Gracie, you need to read on."

"I have always suspected it."

"Lemme see." He snatched the page. "Okay, yeah, she didn't want you but soon got over it. And listen to this, 'now they have sweet little Gracie everyone adores'. What's wrong with that?"

"Everyone adores is not the same as she adores."

"You're making too much out of it. I bet most women feel the same way at first. Even my mother, and I know she loves me."

"She didn't want me."

"This is ridiculous. Your mother is a pain in the neck sometimes, but she certainly loves you." He took hold of my shoulders and gave them a shake. "Read the rest of it! It'll make you forget all about that, I promise you. She walked away with the hat!"

"Walked away with the hat? What do you mean?"

He rattled the pages in front of my face. "Here, see for yourself."

I read the rest of it and stared into space. Obie was right. The sheer weight of her problems made me forget my own. What a fix she'd been in! And, the hat! She kept the officer's hat! That little surprise even pushed her problems out of my head, at least temporarily. The only things left in there were questions—whether it was still around somewhere, whether it could be evidence, whether Aunt Clara's words would hold any weight with the Chief.

"Look at this." Obie pointed to writing scribbled on the back of the last page.

I ran my fingers over the words Aunt Clara had written in heavy black ink: ***In the depths***. Her same slant but sweeping enough to nearly fill the page.

"Wonder what it means?"

"Her state of mind?"

"Maybe. Here's the key from the first vase." Obie folded it into my hand. "Put it somewhere. Taking into account that it was hidden with these pages—"

"If we find the lock it fits, we'll find the hat?"

"That's what I'm thinking. And if we find the hat, it won't do Senator Dollarhide any good at all." Pleased with himself, he leaned down to kiss my 'cute-as-a-button' nose.

When we showed the journal pages to the Chief and told him about the key, his response was predictable. He whistled through his teeth four times and wanted the hat.

"Could you do something with it if we find it?" I asked.

He took a deep breath and let it out in another whistle. "Listen you two, I can't promise anything. But I'd like to set my eyes on it again, have it here on my desk. At least we would have something tangible, something to prop up a dead woman's words. Without it, we got nothing."

Later at home, I could not stop myself from confronting Mother. She was in the kitchen and, from the smell of things, she'd been cooking all afternoon.

"Gracie, you're just in time to set the table," she said, cutting me off before I had a chance to speak. So I set out plates, forks and knives on a once-white linen gone rosy from being washed accidently with my red skirt. When she called dinner, I came to the table with the pages in my hand, proof she didn't want me. And, here, she'd made fried chicken and mashed potatoes and chocolate cake—all my favorites. Proof that she cared?

"What are those?"

"I'll show you in a minute but I have a question first. Did you ... were you happy when you had me?"

She smoothed down her apron and frowned a bit. "Why, yes, I was happy."

"I mean, when you first found out. Did you want me?"

"Of course, I wanted you. What a question. It was just a surprise, that's all."

"Would you rather have had a boy? Did Dad want a boy?"

She narrowed her eyes and gave me the look of suspicion she'd perfected so well. "Grace, are you in trouble?"

"Trouble? You mean ... *that* kind of trouble? Of course not!"

"Then, why all the questions?"

Ah, geez. I handed her the pages to read for herself, which was completely unfair, as though proof of my petty insecurities was the most significant point to be made, when Aunt Clara's words revealed so much more. I felt like a slug in mud afterward.

At the first opportunity, Obie and I went back over to the house in search of the hat. We tried the key from the vase in every lock we saw. We looked in and behind and under and above every piece of furniture, every place big enough to hide a hat. In the kitchen we went through all the cabinets, which was kind of silly. Obie even checked the flour bin, more for a laugh than anything.

"Okay, now what?" I asked.

"What about your grandfather's library?"

"Obie, I seriously doubt Aunt Clara ever went in there."

"But, we might as well look while we're here."

Four long guns locked in a corner cabinet made my boy-friend whistle through his teeth like his father and ask about ownership. I turned my back to him and smiled.

"You take the bookshelves and I'll go through the desk," he said, bouncing into the Judge's leather chair. The desk was locked but the key to it just sat there in an ashtray. He used it and happily began opening drawers.

The Judge's law books filled a whole wall of shelves. I slid one out wondering how many times he'd poured over that very volume on the bench. It was well worn, felt weighty in my hands. And the smell, a deep, olden smell that can't be put into words. Maybe the smell of justice. For the first time, I sensed a connection to the old man who'd never looked my way.

Obie interrupted my thoughts. "Hey, here's something! A cigar box with silver dollars. There must be … let's see … twenty. There's twenty of them. I guess we need to assume they belong to your Uncle Charles."

"Yes, but what about these law books? Do you think they can be mine?"

The only place left was the safe. We searched around for the key and didn't find one. We tried the key from the vase and it didn't fit. After that we sort of gave up, figuring Porter Clark, the family lawyer, had it. We turned to each other and held up empty hands. It was all a big waste of time, just like I figured.

Twelve

On a hot day in early July, Obie and I got to meet Henry for the first time. Mary had already told him about his mother so she introduced me as family, which was a nice way to start. Henry showed us his room, hamster, and baseball cards. Then we all sat at the kitchen table for lemonade. He went away for a minute and came back with a framed picture of three men in Army clothes. He pointed proudly to the one in the middle. "That's my dad, he died last year."

"It was taken in France in 1944, just a month after D-Day," Mary said.

"I'm sorry about your father." I said, rubbing Henry's arm. I needed somehow to touch him. "He was a good man, and a smart one, too."

"How can you tell?"

"Well, for one thing, he picked you for a son."

Henry smiled at that.

"Do you have grandparents?"

The boy looked at Mary and she said, "they died."

"Mine are gone, too. What about aunts and uncles?"

"I have a brother," Mary said. "He's married with two kids, but they live in Minnesota."

I wanted to hug Henry, but settled for resting an arm across his shoulders. "You have another aunt and uncle, my parents. Two uncles, actually. There's Uncle Charles. He's in Korea. Would you like to meet them sometime?"

He nodded. "Do I have another father?"

"Uh, don't know what to tell you about that."

Obie rescued me. "Want to toss the ball around?" Henry's face lit up and out they went.

Mary and I sat back and just smiled at each other. Then, I asked, "How did he take the news?"

"A lot for him to accept at first, but children are resilient. I think, now, he's real pleased. It's good he got to be with her a little bit, even if he didn't know."

"Did he ask questions?"

"You mean, did he ask why?"

"Yeah."

"I imagine those questions will come later." She tilted her head and gazed at me with soft eyes. "Grace, you have been awfully vague about the father. I assume you know who he is."

"Yes, I have the birth certificate. One day soon, I'll take it to the adoption agency for the file. You can see it if you want but … maybe you shouldn't."

"Why not?"

"Then, you'll have to decide whether to tell Henry, and there's no good answer."

"Oh, dear."

"Right now, you can say you don't know and it won't be a lie. Someday, when he's old enough, maybe he'll want the truth and it'll be there for him. I can give him Aunt Clara's journal, too, so he can see it from her side."

The money from Aunt Clara had gone for new brakes on Mary's rusty car, Dad gave me money to buy Henry some shoes, but it was just a band-aid on a fracture. Mary soon got notice of an increase in rent. Obie was of the opinion that the father ought to give a little. It got me to thinking. The man should step up, for once, to do things like buy shoes and pay rent.

All pumped up the next day, I decided to visit William Dollarhide. Frankly, I was operating on pure impulse, and on top of that it was raining, so I should have called it off.

Things started out fine. A bit of luck put me there during his secretary's lunch break, which left him exposed to people like me. I could see him in his private office. The man looked up from reading something, stared for a second, then darted his eyes like a rabbit in a corner. He recovered quickly and came out to greet me with his politician's smile painted on. "You're Bill Dawson's daughter, aren't you?" He knew very well.

"And, Clara Bond's niece."

"Yes, I'm sorry for your loss." Emptiest words I ever heard.

"Thanks," I said as flatly as possible.

"What can I do for you?" He waved me to a chair in his office and sank into a seat behind a ridiculously large desk. He looked so impressive and official there—U.S. flag on one side of him, Commonwealth of Virginia on the other.

His office was what I would call plush—thick rug that swallowed noise, deep cushiony armchairs, fancy oil painting mounted on the wall with a light shining on it. Yes, he could afford to help. I took the plunge. "Your son, the one Clara gave birth to in 1943, is seven years old now and living not two miles from here."

"I didn't–"

"Please, don't deny it. She gave the baby up only out of desperation. You must know that. He's a lovely little boy, I've met him. But, his father has died and his mother is short of money."

"Now, wait a minute–"

"I'm hoping you'll step up to help at this late date."

"Hold on, I don't appreciate this unsubstantiated accusation."

"It's not unsubstantiated. I have the birth certificate."

"Women lie on birth certificates all the time."

"I have Clara's journal account of her desperate situation. And Henry … that's his name, Henry Mullin. He looks just like you, even has your chin dimple."

Dollarhide sat silent. Planning his strategy, no doubt.

"Didn't you ever wonder what happened to him?"

"Look young lady, you're way out of line with this."

"No, I'm not. He's your son, he needs financial support and you can give it to him, simple as that." I made a show of eying his high-priced surroundings.

"If I give him money, it'll be the same as saying I'm the father. I have a position to uphold in this community and, frankly, there's no real proof. Cleft chins are commonplace. And as for the journal, it doesn't mean a thing."

Now, that made me mad. "I know about Donnie Ray Carr." A flash of fear came and went in his eyes. Quick, but I saw it. "Aunt Clara told me just before she died."

"Nobody will believe the rants of a dying woman."

I dug my nails into the chair arms. "There's an account of that, too, in her journal ... details of what happened at the break. Doesn't read like rants. Actually, it's quite convincing." I raised an eyebrow at him.

"Your aunt was a crazy, clinging woman. People will see it that way."

Good thing I didn't have a firearm. "You might be right. I'll turn the journal over to Chief Sayer and we'll find out." It was an empty threat because the Chief already had it, but Dollarhide didn't know that.

He gave me an icy stare. "I suggest you think about what you're doing, Miss Dawson. Think about it very carefully."

We had just traded threats and it was my turn to speak. All I did was narrow my eyes. We both heard the secretary return from lunch. Dollarhide popped from his chair and escorted me out with polite words and a goodbye, treating me like an interested voter. Her timing was perfect for him. Well, maybe for both of us since it kept me from saying anything more.

I know, I know. I shouldn't have gone there and I should not have mentioned Donnie Ray Carr. I didn't intend to but he'd made me so gosh-darned mad! On the other hand, my grandmother once said vinegar draws scum to the surface. She was boiling beef bones for soup at the time, but I think it still fits. Frankly, the mood I was in, I wanted to do more than just threaten him. I won't tell you what I wanted to do because it isn't very nice.

Okay, okay, I'll tell you. I wanted to rip his arm clean out of its socket and bash his head in with it.

The Chief fussed at me for going. He said, "Grace Francis Dawson, you shouldn't have done that!" He'd never called me by my full name before. I didn't even know he knew it. Anyway, it scared the heck out of me and made Obie's eyes bug out. The Chief didn't go on about it anymore, though. That's one of the things I like about him. He tends to speak his mind and then forget it.

This time, however, he switched to another touchy topic, asking again about Donnie Ray's hat. "Does it exist or doesn't it? That's all I want to know. I'm ready to send somebody over to tear the house apart. If it's in there, we'll find it." He stuck a finger in his ear and shook it hard. "All you gotta do is say the word," he added, staring straight at me.

I sat silent, wishing I had a stick of gum. It wasn't that I minded somebody coming to the house. The Chief could come, himself, I told him. But we had already searched, I didn't think it would do any good, and I gotta admit, the phrase, "tear the house apart" worried me because it still belonged to Uncle Charles.

And, speaking of Uncle Charles, just a few days later we got a War Department telegram that Charles Philip Bond had been killed on the USS Everett.

Thirteen

I had come to depend on the prickly willys as a warning, but the truth is, they can't be entirely trusted. They always mean trouble when I do get them, but if I don't it doesn't mean a thing.

Take the morning of Uncle Charles's funeral, for example. The willys definitely let me down that day. There was a snake in my car! A rattlesnake! I mean, is there a situation more in need of warning than that? My hair stands on end now just to think of it—the long skinny thing stretched out in the back window, sunning itself, when Mother and I went to get in. My first hint of trouble was movement from the side of my eye as the snake began to coil. Then it rattled. We gasped at each other from opposite ends of the front seat and leaped out of the car!

Mother bolted to telephone Dad, still turning to him when she needs a man. He came flying. With a stick about as long, he dragged the snake out and flung it across the yard while we cowered. Then he chopped off its head with an axe and that was that.

I had left the windows open again, so he let me have it for the millionth time, said the snake probably dropped from the tree overhead and slithered in. He wondered out loud if this would finally cure me. Oh yes! I told him. But the reason he'd always given was possible rain. Not enough of a motivator, I guess. Neither were a few other intruders—wasps and bees, even a chipmunk once. But a rattlesnake? I promised to never leave the windows open again.

We went ahead with my uncle's funeral without his body. A funeral without a body was nearly normal during the war. I can still remember Caleb Sayer's funeral—Mrs. Sayer hiding behind a veil, the Chief, his shoulders quivering as he cried into his sleeve. Obie and I were eleven then and did not like each other. He'd stuffed a frog down my dress at the county fair and I was still angry about it. Even so, it was saddening to see him slumped down in the front pew like that between his brokenhearted parents.

Anyway, it was just my mother and me for the reading of Uncle Charles's will. It had been only two months since we'd done the same for Aunt Clara. Porter Clark said I needed to be there for this one, too, which seemed odd because I barely knew my uncle. He'd always been gone—first the big war, then Korea. The gap between the wars had been filled with career Navy, a ploy to keep from coming home, Mother said.

I hope to one day have an office as nice as Porter Clark's. An entire wall of windows, armchairs deep and cushiony like Dollarhide's, a conference table large enough to seat eight, on top of a rug big enough to cover the whole floor.

Mother and I chose the armchairs. She reached over to brush the hair back from my face, something she had always done and I never minded.

Porter Clark, our short, balding, cheerful lawyer with a red bowtie and protruding Adam's apple, rushed in with a folder, dropped into his chair, pulled out a pack of cigarettes and smiled at us from across the desk. "Well, well. Here we are again." He managed to hold the smile even while he talked, a valuable skill for a lawyer. "We seem to be running low on heirs in this family, the loss of three in as many years."

"And you almost lost the rest of us this morning," Mother said. She proceeded to tell him about the snake, overdoing it in my opinion. It was never a real danger, thanks to Dad.

Mr. Clark took a cigarette and lit it. "I'm certainly glad it turned out that way," he said, puffing smoke. "Let me start by saying we made two attempts to contact Charles about Clara's death. But, communications from a destroyer being what they are, I don't know if we succeeded. We never heard anything." He tapped the folder in front of him. "This is his will, dated almost three years ago, shortly after the Judge's death. Unless another surfaces in a reasonable time period, this document will stand. I don't expect one. Charles never married as far as I know, and last time we talked, which was sometime in the winter, he was still a confirmed bachelor."

"Charles didn't think much of marriage. No surprise after living with our parents," Mother said.

"Perhaps the next generation will make out better." Mr. Clark flashed his smile and nodded at me. "Grace, as you'll see, the death of your Uncle Charles affects you more than anyone." Then, he opened the folder and read the will out loud. Even with all its complicated phrases, it had a simple message: Charles had left everything to Clara.

The lawyer stared at me like he expected a reaction but I was slow to catch on. In fact, he had to explain it, which shows I have a lot to learn about the law. "Grace, as Clara's sole and legal heir, everything that belonged to Charles now passes to you. And since Judge Bond had bequeathed all to Charles … basically, everything belonging to the Judge three years ago now belongs to you. One never knows how things will turn out, and I see it all in my business." He turned his smile on Mother. "Evelyn, I know why Charles did this. He never worried about you financially like he did Clara."

To her credit, my mother seemed genuinely pleased for me, no sign of annoyance or resentment at being passed over. Just a nod and a smile. Me? I was afraid to smile, fearing it would be a goofy one.

"It is not a tremendous amount," Mr. Clark continued, "includes the house on Smoketown Road and all its contents, $1000 in a savings account, stocks and bonds valued at an estimated $5000 in the safe deposit box at the bank. There would have been more but, shortly after the Judge's death, Charles took $30,000 and invested it. Something speculative, I fear, but that's only a guess. The Judge had kept a tight rein, cautious about the stock market after the crash of '29. So Charles went a little crazy with his abrupt financial freedom."

A sudden burst of maturity caused me to sit up straighter in my chair. "Not a great fortune, Grace, but what's left of the family estate has taken a free fall and landed at your feet. Not too bad for someone your age. You can sell the house, or live in it when the time comes. You and your mother can work that out."

"It won't be for a while yet," Mother said, reaching to smooth back my hair again.

With that comment my sense of maturity shrank. I didn't mind, though. At least she was smiling.

"I recommend you use some of the funds to keep up the house," Mr. Clark said. "Silas Trent can be a big help in that department. Have you seen him around?"

"No, not since Aunt Clara died." But I'd seen Silas at the house before, fixing things in overalls that bulged at the sides because his pockets were full of tools.

"I'll ask him to resume his job as caretaker. And one last thing … you don't have a will, Grace, as far as I know. Under your changed circumstances, strictly from a legal standpoint, my advice is to come in and make one."

I had often dreamed as a kid of following a trail of shiny coins that led to a mountain of quarters behind a bush. Made me wonder if the dream finally came true with this surprise inheritance.

Good thing school was out for the summer. All I wanted to do was think about that money and how to spend it. I could help Henry myself with the very money intended for his real mother. No more looking to William Dollarhide for his support. Plus, I could pay for my own college and buy a new bathing suit.

And the house! The first thing Obie and I did over there was wind all the clocks to get them started, bring the place back to life. It didn't take long after that for us to plan how we would live there one day. "Five big bedrooms! What'll we do with all the space?" I said, laughing. "I guess we'll need to fill it up with kids."

"Fine with me. Can we start on that now?" Obie grabbed me around the waist and pulled me to him.

I knew he was mostly kidding. What a great thing, though, to have such a house for the future.

Obie said, "The Judge's bedroom is the largest, with its own bathroom. Seems like we ought to have that one for ourselves. Think you could stand being in there once we clear it all out?"

"Maybe, if we paint the walls, get a new rug, and of course a new bed."

"Don't see why not. We'll have the money."

Somehow, hearing Obie talk about the money woke me up. I held out my hands. "Wait a second. Is any of this mine? Shouldn't it all go to Henry?"

Obie gave me a blank stare and then a frown. "Oh, I see what you mean." He held out his hands, too. "You need to discuss this with your dad."

Turned out, my father had some definite opinions. "Clara drew up a will and made you her beneficiary. Legally, you can do what you want."

"But is legal always right?"

"Hardly. Sometimes, it's up to rational people to help the law along."

"Well, I want to do what's right and I'm afraid it means giving Henry everything, including the house."

"Once the funds are released, you can do that. But not the house."

"No?"

"The house has been in this family for ... well ... you make the fourth generation. You are a grandchild, Henry is a grandchild, the only two there will ever be."

"Then, what should I do?"

"You could sell it and split the proceeds, but selling the house out of the family was never anybody's intention. You need to retain ownership. And about the money ... I don't think you should just give it all to Mary Mullin. We can't be sure of her level of know-how or discipline when it comes to money. Maybe you should put it in a savings account to earn interest and send her something each month to make things easier."

"I feel like a worm. All I've been thinking about is how to spend the money myself."

"How would you spend it?"

I told him.

"I'll pay for college like we planned, but there's nothing wrong with making changes to the house. And go ahead, buy yourself that bathing suit." He was obviously amused.

I saw nothing amusing about the desperate need for a new bathing suit but I let it go. "Live-in college?" I asked. Silly question.

"Of course, live-in college. Where else? Grace, have you thought about simply moving Henry and his mother into the house from that sad little rental?"

I'm sure my eyebrows shot up. "Wow, what a great idea!"

"Think about it first, before you offer."

"I don't need to think about it. What a great idea!"

"Gracie, don't be so impulsive, you need to give it careful thought. Once they're in there, they're in there for good. You will be away at school four years or more, but after that you'll probably want to get married and live there yourself. You'll want it to be your house."

"Yeah, but it's a big house, Dad, plenty of room."

Fourteen

The next day saw us making another try for the hat. Buster and Blue were with Obie when he picked me up, even though it looked like rain. I sat sideways on the seat to watch them in the back. I swear to you, those dogs were smiling.

As we approached the house I felt something wrong, and knew it for sure getting out of the truck. Goosebumps, arm hairs at attention, rapid pulse, tingling between my eyebrows, the whole set of symptoms. I took it all out on the gum in my mouth, but the symptoms worsened on the sidewalk and the dogs picked up on it. "Obie, something isn't right …"

Silas Trent came barreling around the corner of the house waving his arms and met us on the front porch. "Got something to say before you set foot in there. I come by to fix the back-porch screen door and found two fellas ransacking the house."

"Who were they?" Obie asked.

"Never seen either of 'em before, or the car they come in. They looked mean and dumb as stumps, both of 'em."

"What kind of car?"

"A '47 Dodge, black." Obie cautiously opened the door. "Don't worry, they're gone. I scared 'em off, but it's a mess in there."

We stood in the doorway and looked. Plants and vases overturned, books scattered, drawers dumped out, pictures knocked off the walls or crooked. The dogs broke passed us and busied themselves sniffing.

"They've been searching in here," Obie said. "Wait 'til Pop sees."

"Dollarhide, it has to be."

"Some of his hires, more like."

"Obie, they busted the urn in the corner. I really liked that urn." The jade box had been knocked on the floor, Charles's letters spilling out on the rug. I gathered them up and slid them in my purse.

We checked in the Judge's library. The silver dollars were gone from the desk, gun cabinet smashed and emptied. And, they'd broken into the safe!

"Gosh, Obie, what if they found the hat?" Fear gripped me.

"Do you think it was in the safe? I thought you said Aunt Clara wouldn't put anything in there."

"That's right."

"Did you tell Dollarhide about the hat?"

"Of course not."

"Well then, they didn't know about it. They were probably searching for the journal you threatened him with. A lucky

114

break for us that Pop still has it. And speaking of Pop, this is really gonna piss him off."

The rest of the house appeared untouched. "It looks like they didn't get far in their search," I said.

"Which means they might come back. We'll leave the dogs here overnight. Neither of them could bite their way through a biscuit, but at least they'll raise a ruckus if anybody tries to get in. And this time, we'll lock the doors."

We set out bowls of water and made a move to leave. The dogs tore into the front hall ahead of us, all legs and paws trying to find traction on the polished floor. Eager to get out, they crowded around Obie as he went to open the door. He pointed a finger. "No, you boys. Stay."

Both dogs sighed like people, collapsed on the floor and stared up at us with the saddest eyes, as near to pouting as dogs can get.

I didn't sleep well that night—asleep and awake, asleep and awake—skipping across the hours like one of Obie's creek pebbles. When I woke up at five it wasn't light yet but the stars had gone. I lay there uneasy, listening for noises, heard nothing but crickets and a far-off train. I slipped out of bed and padded down the hall to check on Mother. Nothing amiss there, I could tell by her breathing that she was deep in sleep. But something was wrong somewhere. The willys never lied when they came.

More sleep would have been impossible so I made the bed, straightened the room, dressed for the day, spruced up my old oxfords, played at reorganizing my closet, ate a quick bowl of cornbread and milk, and forced myself to wait until seven to leave. I heard Mother stirring but left the house without saying goodbye.

On one hand, it was early to show up at Obie's. On the other hand, Mrs. Sayer was already working in the kitchen. I could smell her biscuits. She answered the door, surprised to see me, and called up the stairs to Obie. "Why the knock?" she asked, rubbing me on the arm. "Want some breakfast?"

"Smells real good, but no thanks." I followed her to the kitchen and took a seat at the table while she poured coffee into my favorite cup. "Sorry about the time but Obie said he'd be up at the crack of dawn."

"The crack of noon, more like," she said, winking. "The Chief's already eaten and gone. We got a call at an outlandish hour, woke us both up. Something about a drunk breaking windows."

Obie appeared with tousled hair, tucking a shirt into his pants. "What's the matter?" He looked at me with concern.

I don't tell many people about my premonitions, afraid they'd think me either a tomfool or a fibber. Wasn't sure yet what to expect from his parents, so I just said, "Thought you wanted to get an early start."

"Yeah, but ..." He glanced at the clock. "I mean, it's okay. You just never got here this early before."

While Obie wolfed bacon and eggs and then filled his mother's wood box enough to last the whole day, I glanced at Sunday's funny papers, wrapped hair nervously around my finger, and listened to the motor of their cat curled up on a rug.

Afterward, going down the porch steps, Obie grabbed my arm. "You show up real early and you're twisting your hair. What's the matter?"

"Don't know, exactly. I think there's something wrong at the house."

"But the dogs are there," Obie said, picking up on my worry.

When we turned onto Smoketown Road, even before the house appeared through the crabapple trees, we could hear a dog howling.

"It's Buster," Obie said, speeding up.

"He's not happy, that's for sure." I couldn't tell one howl from another but trusted that Obie knew.

"The question is why Buster's making a racket and Old Blue's not saying a word." The hair on my arms bristled, almost to the point of uncomfortable. I rubbed them both up and down. Obie noticed but didn't say anything.

Buster met us at the door and kept on howling, even as Obie rubbed his head and whispered, "It's okay boy, settle down, settle down. Where's Blue?"

Side-stepping them, I went into the parlor and saw it immediately. Across the room, another rattlesnake! My first reaction was panic, I might have yelled out. But it was limp as a wet mop, clearly dead. And a few feet away, hidden behind a chair, Old Blue lay just as limp, just as dead.

Silas arrived about that time and whistled long and low. "Poor fella, poor old fella," he said when he saw Blue. "That's a shittin' shame, a damn shittin' shame. They come in the back, the glass is busted. The same two, I reckon." He

117

helped us load the animals in the truck, including the snake in a burlap sack, then he stood in the street watching us sling gravel.

Obie flew to the nearest vet man, cutting a fifteen-minute trip down to ten. We were lucky the doc was there, since his practice mainly involved house calls on horses and cows. He examined Buster first and declared him okay. Then, he looked at the other two and pieced together what probably happened. The battered snake was attacked by both dogs but still managed to sink its fangs into Blue at least three times. "When you've got rattlesnake bites and time clicking by with no treatment, it never goes good," the vet man said.

I felt gosh-awful and I know Obie felt worse. I want to say he was angry and inconsolable, but is it possible to be both those things at the same time? Whatever he felt, it hit hard. He was rough on his father later in the day, even spoke with a rudeness I'd never heard before. "You're the law in this town! Can't you do something?"

"Yes, and while I'm the law, we're going to stick to the law."

"But that damn Dollarhide killed Old Blue!"

"The situation is clear as river mud, son. And watch your language around Grace."

Obie looked at me and mouthed, "Sorry."

"I agree that Dollarhide probably hired who did this—"

"Probably?"

"Yes, and he probably arranged for that snake in Grace's car." The Chief cut his eyes at me. "At this point, all we've got are a bunch of probablys. We're looking for the car Silas described—"

Obie threw up his hands. "Is that the best you can do?"

Storm clouds appeared on the Chief's face. "What. You expect special treatment? Is that it?! You expect me to haul Dollarhide in here because you believe his roughnecks killed your dog." He pounded the desk and then clenched his fists to keep from doing it again. "You want me to do something? Then, bring me evidence of a crime, for God's sake! Bring me the damned hat!"

"You'll be able to do something if we find it?" I asked this timidly, afraid to press.

"That is not the point. The point is, I can't do anything without it."

Obie stayed mad at his father all day.

"He was just being realistic," I later offered in the Chief's defense, "and he was trying his best not to irritate you."

"I know that. I found it irritating."

Fifteen

By the next morning, Obie felt sorry about his father. The Chief felt sorry, too, apparently, because he left Obie in charge at the station while he and Ernie came to inspect the mess in the house and take photographs. After they finished, Silas helped me straighten up the place and we made a list of things that needed fixing. It took the remainder of my day. Obie spent the rest of his pulling weeds in the vegetable garden.

That night, to get my mind on something else, I read a few of Uncle Charles's letters to Aunt Clara. I hadn't really known my uncle and now I never would. His words, though, were windows into the man, his concern for her. Take a look at this one:

June 17, 1948

Dear Clara,

I hope this letter finds you well. You seemed so beaten down at the funeral. I'm afraid the burden of the old man took a special toll on you. He messed with all of us – drove Mother to her grave, Evelyn married at nineteen just to run away. Getting drafted was my escape. I regret making it permanent but, in my defense, his tight control invaded every part of my life while all you girls ever got was stony silence as long as you behaved.

Maybe you can be happy now, find a nice man to marry like Evelyn did. You deserve it. The house belongs to me, as does everything the Judge willed forward, but you can live there permanently, consider it yours. Make changes, get rid of those heavy drapes, ask Silas to cut back the bushes to let in some more light. And for heaven's sake, clear out everything that belonged to him. It'll be different then, you'll see.

I'm sending you this little jade box for your treasures. I got it in Japan. Remember how we liked to hide things? Gave us the illusion of control, I guess. Think of me when you use it.

Please forgive me, Charles

I thought for sure Aunt Clara would have told him her secrets, but this letter proved different. He obviously blamed himself and the Judge for her unhappiness. And maybe I was making too much out of it, but that part about liking to hide things gave me hope for the hat.

The next letter, though, brought definite hope, all kinds of hope. Reading it, I whistled in a way my mother would call undignified and began to grin.

February 4, 1951

Dear Clara,

I've been in Wilmington since September, leaving for Korea tomorrow, assigned to USS Everett. It might be a while before I write again. Just so you know, my will leaves everything to you. Evelyn can take care of herself. I made some investments with a chunk of the Judge's money. Porter Clark wouldn't have approved so I kept it from him. The certificates are in the old trunk in the fort, along with that sack of silver dollars. Remember how we stole them one by one from the old man's desk and he never noticed? The trunk is locked up tight, but you remember where we kept the key. Write me care of Everett. I'll write again when I can. Please be happy.

Love, Charles

You gotta admit, it's a peach of a letter. I wanted to get Obie on the telephone right then and read it to him but it was almost midnight and a sleepy old Chief might have answered. So, playing it safe, I left the Sayers alone and waited until morning.

Just like the other day, I got there early enough to force Obie out of bed. Not yet awake, running a hand through his hair, he slid into his seat at the kitchen table, looked pointedly at the clock and frowned at me.

I handed him the folded letter. "Read this."

"It better be good," he said with a sigh.

The Chief walked in around that time carrying an empty cup. He pulled a screwdriver out of his pocket and set it on the table, took his chair and winked at me. He studied his son. "Well, grumpy, what are your plans for today?"

123

Obie didn't answer, eyes on the letter.

"You need to devote at least part of it to helping your mother. She'll tell you what to do."

Mrs. Sayer refilled the Chief's coffee cup, poured some for Obie and me, and pushed the cream and sugar our way. "The beans ought to be picked," she said.

"I can help," I offered, forgetting our own bean crop that needed the same thing.

Obie jerked his head up, completely awake, and waved the letter. "Geez, Pop, wait 'til you read this!"

It only took a second for the Chief to read it while we all looked on. His reaction was underwhelming. "Forts, trunks. Sounds like a couple of kids."

"But, they *were* a couple of kids back then," I said. "And if the grownup Aunt Clara wanted to hide the hat, stands to reason she'd put it right in there with the rest."

The Chief gave a few slow nods. "Okay, can't argue with that." He stood from his chair, drained his cup and grabbed the screwdriver. "All right, go on over there and see what you can find. The beans can wait." He nodded again and kept nodding as he went out the back door.

"Have you heard anything about a fort?" Obie asked.

"No, never heard anything about a fort."

"When I think of a kid's fort, I picture a treehouse. Could there be a treehouse somewhere?"

"I don't think so. But, would a trunk be in a treehouse?"

"Okay, the cellar, then. Kids build forts in cellars."

Heaven knows, we had good reason to search the cellar. We went down the dark, narrow steps with flashlights and new curiosity. I felt like Nancy Drew in *The Hidden Staircase,* shining a light into every cobwebby corner. Spiders scurried except for the ones curled up dead. But not so bad, this cellar, now that it was mine. Only the necessary utilities, though. No trunks, no signs of a fort.

"The attic?" Obie suggested on our way back to the first floor. "An attic seems a more likely place for a trunk."

"Yeah, I had a dream once of finding an old attic trunk filled with gold coins and jewels. Probably right after I read *Ali Baba.*"

Obie chuckled. "I guess every kid dreams something like that. In my dream, I pried open the lid and found a skeleton."

"You would. Did the lid creak?"

"What?"

"In your dream. Did the trunk lid creak when you opened it?"

"Yeah, did yours?"

"Yep, I bet trunk lids always creak, no matter if it's in a dream or a movie or the real thing. Do you think there's any meaning to our dreams?"

"What kind of meaning?"

"Oh, I don't know … maybe that I'd find wealth and you'd find adventure."

On the second floor we found the dusty stairs to the attic. It looked promising at first. Old furniture aplenty, crates and crocks and hat boxes to peer in and through and around. But nothing even close to a fort or a trunk, and it was hot up there.

We went to the kitchen for cold tea made the day before. I poured us each a glass and we sat at the table to cool off. "Know what I think?" I asked.

"What?"

"This whole thing, this hunting for a trunk in a fort … it's a lot like the dreams we had. I agree with your father. It just seems like a game for kids."

On Thursday, I happened to be at the house when Silas Trent came by to repair the gun cabinet and the glass on the back door. "Now that you own this place," he said, scratching a red blotch on his cheek, "I hope you'll get your mind on what all needs to be done around here. The Judge always kept things up but Miss Clara never cared."

"What needs to be done besides the stuff on our list?"

"I got a whole other list."

"Does it include cutting back the bushes?"

"No, the Judge wanted 'em big. And like I said, Miss Clara never cared. But I reckon it can be done now, if you want."

"What's on *your* list, then?"

"Painting, for starters, a lot of painting. Front porch needs scraped and painted, back porch, too. And the outbuildings, they always get passed over. The gardener's shed needs it bad, and the caretaker's cottage."

"Caretaker's cottage?"

"Well, it ain't used for that no more. Ain't had a live-in caretaker for twenty-five years."

"What's it used for now?"

"Nothing much. Charles and Clara played in there as kids. Now, it's mostly just a place for junk. But don't you still think it ought to be kept up?"

"Is there a trunk?"

He paused. "Well, I reckon so, lots of stuff in there."

Bingo! I was beginning to like this man.

Well, I knew about the shed but, in all those times at the house as a child, I had never seen the cottage. Guess I wasn't one to explore too far beyond my nose. In my defense, trees shield it from the house and an overgrown path you would never notice leads to it from the back lawn.

Silas was right, it needed paint. And a new set of shutters. It had a low front door and a low ceiling to match, not a place for the likes of Obie. Poor light inside, couldn't see a thing at first. Heavy drapes and bushes were not the problem here, though. It was more a lack of windows, and the ones it had were dirty.

Silas propped the door open to let in the sun. I was then able to see a stone fireplace across a cluttered floor, gun rack mounted above it without any guns. Kitchen was over toward the right—woodstove against a sooty wall, tarnished pans hanging from the ceiling on a rack. Like Silas said, the cottage had become a storage place for junk, especially near the front door: a cane chair with a hole in the seat, what looked to me like outdated farm equipment, rusty tools and other castoffs.

"Where's the trunk?" I asked.

"Well, I reckon there's at least two. Is this a trunk, would you say?" He took a few steps and rested a hand on what I'd call a cedar chest. Lifting the lid was no trouble. It was filled to the top with old quilts. Quite a find, considering that I love quilts, and these were mine.

"Uncle Charles wrote about an old trunk in a fort. I need to find it."

"Fort? Must be talking about over there," he said, pointing to a far left corner with his lips curled in a smile.

Weaving my way in that direction, I sensed something. It was a cleared out place amongst the clutter, a kind of room, its boundaries formed by piled up furniture—a sideboard, roll-top desk, tall cabinet. A porch swing with the chains still on it rested firmly on two bedside tables, a couple of dusty pillows making a decent place to sit. A rickety table and a rug on the floor were attempts to cozy it up. Somebody, probably Uncle Charles, had written THE ALAMO in big block letters directly on the wall. And on a splintery board nailed next to it: MEMBERS ONLY, KEEP OUT.

Oh, yes, this was definitely something. There was a trunk, an old steamer. Judging by the stickers, it had made its way to Europe and back more than once. It was locked, of course. Silas stood beside me, hands on his hips, watching.

"Any idea where the key is?" I asked.

"Now, that I don't know," he said, scratching at the red place on his cheek.

"Maybe I do. Stay here, if you wouldn't mind." I guess my next actions are easy to predict. With excitement and high energy I scooted to the house, fished that key from the vase out of Aunt Clara's jewelry chest and hurried back.

The key actually opened that rusty old lock, but not from the get-go. Silas had to squirt machine oil into the keyhole first. The lid creaked as Silas drew it up, causing me to grin wide and regret Obie not being there.

But, sifting through the contents, my excitement faded fast. Yes, stock certificates—official-looking envelopes with a number stamped on the front, each of them sealed. And, yes, silver dollars in a drawstring bag from the bank. A few other items, too, a baseball, old erector set, spark plugs. Spark plugs? And a crowbar, of all things. But no hat, or anything belonging to Aunt Clara. I'd been so certain moments before. Now what? I'll tell you what. I went home to sulk.

Sixteen

The following evening before the sun set, I was back at the cottage, this time with a crowd. Obie and Silas, and even my father, showed up out of a personal interest to find the hat. Ernie Reed, too, sent by the Chief. We looked through the trunk again, as though the rest thought Silas and I might have missed something.

Then Dad asked, "Why did you think the hat was in the trunk?"

"Well, Uncle Charles locked stuff away in there. We were hoping Aunt Clara had done the same."

"And she gave no hint in the journal?"

"No. See for yourself. Read the last page." I handed my father the bundle.

He read it and nodded. "What about these words on the outside, *In the Depths*."

"I figure she meant her state of mind."

"Perhaps, but what if we consider a more literal interpretation. Is there a basement in this place?"

We all looked at Silas. He shook his head and told us it was built on a slab.

"Isn't there a cellar in the main house?" Ernie asked.

"We already looked, but I guess we can look again," Obie said.

"Let's finish here first," Dad said. "There was a case last year in Roanoke. A guy hid $20,000 from a bank heist under the floorboards of his house. Looks like this is a wide-plank floor …"

Every eye looked down. Obie and Ernie shoved the trunk out of the way and slid the rug back. "What about this plank here, looks kind of loose," Ernie said. He tried to lift it with the tips of his fingers but he hurt one of them and stuck it in his mouth.

"The crowbar," Dad suggested. We all talked at once, saying it was probably in the trunk for that very purpose. The plank, about two feet long, came up with no trouble then. Clearly, it had been lifted before.

"Gimme the flashlight," Ernie said. He took it from Obie and shined it around. "Nothing much in here except, well, there's a paper sack." He reached in. "Something is sure in it." When he gave it to me, I knew what it was by the feel. As I pulled Donnie Ray's long-lost officer's hat out of the bag, in fine condition except for a little dirt, the sight of it made me cry.

Obie and Ernie laughed their sides off, carried on and cavorted, kicking up dust on the floor. The mood must have been catching. Silas joined them without knowing why, and even my father laughed out loud and gave me a rough hug. His serious side soon returned, however. He relocked the trunk, placed the key in the palm of my hand and folded my fingers over it. "What's left in there looks valuable. Keep it locked."

When we recovered, we all had the same idea. "Just wait 'til Pop sees!" Obie hollered, first to say it out loud.

Nobody wanted to miss the big moment so it took all of us in a four-vehicle caravan to deliver the prize. We trooped into the Chief's office making a lot of racket and I set the hat down on his desk before he could complain.

"Well, I'll be damned, there it is!" he crowed, surprise and pleasure popping out on his face. He picked it up and turned it this way and that. "It's something I never expected to see again. His hat, all right, his number's in it. Tremendous find!"

"Now that you've got it, Pop, what are you gonna do with it?"

"Hell, I don't know. Nothing I'd like better than to put Dollarhide away for a good long time. The journal claims he shoved Donnie Ray over the edge and then pushed the bike over from twenty feet away. That means it was a deliberate act, and he decided right then to cover it up." The Chief waved the journal pages at my father. "Have you read these, Bill?"

Dad nodded.

"What's your opinion? Do you think this case is worth prosecuting?"

"You'll probably lose, but I think you ought to try."

"Would you prosecute it?"

Dad grinned. "Is that rhetorical or are you asking me to take the case?"

"Guess I'm asking. But only if we can find the body and bike, and only if we can prove identity. Those are big ifs, I know, but we don't have a prayer without them."

"Chances are slim, regardless. Dollarhide will hire a team of fancy lawyers who could draw the case out for months. Not looking forward to that. But it'll cause quite a scandal in the newspapers, could wreck all his plans for reelection next year. Might be worth it."

"Is that a yes?"

"Let me think about it a day or two."

"Pop, when you go in for the body, can I go with you?" Obie asked.

"Hell, no. Why would you want to? Nobody sane would volunteer. It'll be a helluva job to find that body, going in from the side. I dread it."

"We've got one thing going for us," Ernie said. "At least the break won't be packed with snow in July."

A lot happened the following week. Tuesday, the Chief and Ernie, plus a photographer from the Betula Bulletin, hiked into the break while the rest of us sat on our hands.

Obie and I went back to the cottage. In all the excitement, we'd forgotten about the trunk and the valuable-looking stuff inside. We naturally understood the value of the silver dollars. The stock certificates were a different matter, though. When we opened the first envelope and pulled out the certificate, the main points were plain: Colgate, 1000 shares, issued on September 14, 1949. The next envelope: Coca-Cola, 500,

September 17, 1949. We had no idea of the value but it soon turned into fun, discovering the famous names I now owned a piece of.

Altogether, there was stock from ten companies, two I'd never even heard of: E Everett Sloane and International Business Machines. One envelope looked quite different and, wasn't a stock certificate at all. It looked like a deed to property in Abingdon Virginia, an hour or so from Betula.

I left the coins in the trunk, relocked it, and took the rest home. That evening I made a tidy list of the stock on a piece of lined paper, and the next day put it all in a satchel and carried it to Dad. I set the certificates in the middle of his desk and handed him the list. "Gracie, my girl, you might have something here."

"Any idea what they're worth?"

"No, you'll need a stockbroker for that. I'll make a call and line one up. One thing's for sure. Your Uncle Charles knew the value of diversifying."

"And here's something else," I said, fishing in the satchel for the other envelope. "Appears to be a deed."

He pulled the paper out and studied it. He looked sleepy but I knew he was absorbing every word. "I'll be damned, this is an office building. I know the very one. It's small, but right there on Route 11 across from the Dogwood Motel. Looks like he paid a flat ten grand for it, an excellent price. That new interstate highway is slated to come right through Abingdon. You could sell the building now for more like fifteen, and the value will only go up.

Seventeen

The search party returned after three long days. They came out with a body and a motorcycle, along with photographs of the scene as first discovered, which apparently agreed with Aunt Clara's journal—both Donnie Ray and his bike had gone over the edge, and he had gone over first. They said the body was mostly a skeleton but parts of the uniform were still recognizable, including a piece of shirt with a badge hanging on it.

Big news in Betula, spreading fast and far on the street. People said finding Officer Carr's body after that much time was the weightiest story the town had seen since Pearl Harbor back in 1941. And when the Chief linked William Dollarhide to the crime, charged him with manslaughter and hauled him right off Main Street in broad daylight, the news went state wide, maybe even further.

My father agreed to take the case. Dollarhide did not bring in a team of lawyers as expected, but hired only one man, Canby Kluth. Dad said this man would be enough. He had already seen Kluth in action once, when the shrewd lawyer delayed a case for a year and then won it with a surprise acquittal. Kluth's first action the day he blew into our town was to get Dollarhide released on bail.

I met with the stockbroker the following week. Dad was already too busy to go, so I went alone. The man, Sturgill was his name, had red hair and freckles, talked too fast and said too much, but here are the main points: Only one stock was worthless, the rest were solid and desirable to own. Some paid regular dividends. Altogether, they were worth fifty-thousand dollars, give or take, at the last closing bell. I should count myself lucky and not sell any of them in this healthy bull market, whatever that meant.

When Dad heard, he suggested I put it all in a trust to be split down the middle with Henry. "If your luck holds out, you both could be set for a comfortable life."

>*>*>*<*<*<

Our wait for the trial to begin can be measured by my last year of high school. That's about how long it took. However, I associate the start of senior year with another thing, entirely. The final acceptance that my parents were finished. Up until then there'd always been reasons to hope. Neither had remarried, for one thing. They still haven't. Dad sends money every month. The court ordered him to do it but he doesn't seem to mind, and Mother tends to soften each time a check shows up without her having to nag. This alone had given me hope and I always thought it was Mother who needed to give in.

But, during an honest discussion the night before school started, I asked my father what the chances were. He just smiled, said he'd had his fill of fighting—with people from foreign countries, and my mother. Any fight left was reserved for the courtroom.

So, it's clearly too late for my mother. Dad has moved on. He seems content to occasionally call on the same woman, a placid, long-haired widow of the war. Mother wants me to dislike her but I don't. The years since the war have turned Dad colorful, growing his hair longer than mine and pulled back in a ponytail, and he's grown a long mustache, too.

He's happy now to work all week, fish on weekends, and as autumn changes the look of the trees, get on his motorcycle and zoom about the countryside on freshly-paved roads smooth as ribbons, the tails of his mustache whipping in the wind. They talk about him in town. The women, I mean. Unmarried men his age are scarce as palm trees around here. I think they'd all like to climb behind him on that bike and take a ride.

On Thanksgiving, the Sayers invited Mother and me for dinner. Now, that was fun. Our contributions, a three-layer chocolate cake and pumpkin pie. When we got there, Obie came downstairs dressed in boots and jeans under a jacket and tie. He often shows up like that on Sundays. The women at church don't like it much, but I sure do. His mother didn't say anything, with us being there, but she gave him a look. My mother would have given him a look, too, if I hadn't looked at her first. The Chief stayed out of it, I noticed, and other than that touchy moment, we had a fine time.

The Monday after Thanksgiving, hunting season officially began. Obie skipped school to hunt deer with his dad, his Uncle Jubal and cousin George. I guess the importance of an education has its limits, even in the Chief's mind.

They like to hunt, my father likes to fish. Seems like every man in Betula does one or the other, or both. Dad was a hunter before the war, and afterward vowed to never take up a gun again. That's why, the fishing. People don't shoot fish with guns.

Early December brought the kind of cold and wind that usually waits for February. Sometimes it was bad enough that we passed each other on the street without saying a word. Christmas Eve and Christmas Day came with snow so deep that nobody could visit and we had to stay home. It was just me and Mother the entire time, when Christmasing with Obie was all I really wanted to do.

With just the two of us, though, she was feeling fairly mellow, the distance between us smaller and safer, as flying snow blocked the front door.

"Were you ever happy with Dad?" I took the opportunity to ask over a bowl of popcorn.

"Well, yes, in the beginning. But, I should have known better than to marry him. His father was a cheater and men always take after their dads."

"Grandpa Dawson was a cheater?" An image flashed from years before of the kind grandfather who smiled at me with my daddy's eyes and smelled like pipe tobacco. "I never heard that," I said with a frown, doubting.

"It was before you were even born. Everybody knew it."

"Have you ever heard about Chief Sayer cheating?" I was leaving myself wide open here.

"No, never heard anything about him. I guess that means you're safe."

Mother was being soft-hearted with that statement and I grinned at her in appreciation. She knows I plan to marry Obie, I've told her more than once. Luckily, she's fond of him. Both my parents like him, which makes things so much easier.

But Mother has strong opinions on how things ought to work and she voiced them all that day. "You should wait until after college to marry," she said, probably afraid we'll rush into a wedding because of my 'financial windfall' as she calls it.

"We *are* going to wait," I said.

"You might discover that you and Obie were just a high school crush."

"No, we won't."

"Your feelings might dwindle, or one of you could meet somebody else."

"They won't, and we won't."

"You say that now but you never know. If it's the real thing, it'll still be there in four years."

Yeah, yeah, yeah, yeah. I'd already told her we were going to wait. What more did she want? I know I should be grateful to her for all she's done—and I am, I am, of course I am—but, geez! The plain truth is, there'll never be anyone else but Obie for me.

I get it, though. Mother's marriage didn't work out and she's trying to keep me from the same fate. She figures hers was a mistake, she picked the wrong man. Well, if she did, I'm grateful. I can't imagine having anyone else for a dad.

Hmm, here's a question. If she'd married another man and given me a different dad, would I still be me? Just how does that work? I pondered it for about five seconds and then went to put another log on the fire. It required too much deep thinking and I was on Christmas vacation.

Mother still rehashes the same old hurts, probably always will. I believe, when she gets like that, she might even resent those regular checks because they cut down on her right to complain. Gosh, just listen to me. Even now, I tend to blame her for all their problems, and it isn't fair. Dad was the one who cheated. I want to say she probably drove him to it, but is there ever a reason valid enough for doing that?

By New Year's Eve the snow had gone so Obie and I, together, opened the door on 1952.

An early spring meant a break from snowed-over roads and fly-away hair. And it meant another trip to Norton for me. Two reasons. First, to settle Henry's birth certificate in the official file where it belonged. Second, to buy a dress for the prom before they were all picked over.

Girls in Betula wear white for senior prom, and the same dress again for Graduation. Very economical. One girl last year got three wears out of hers, putting it on one more time to get married in a month later. I thought she was carrying economy too far.

It has been that way forever, this wearing o' the white. There's a photograph from 1932, of Mother in her white prom dress made of lace. She still has that dress, and her wedding dress as well, both tucked carefully in tissue paper, in the cedar chest, in our dusty attic. I once worried she'd try to force that prom dress on me, but I have my own money now for dresses, don't even need to involve my dad.

The night before the train to Norton I had a crazy dream. All the clothes in my closet had gone greenish in a matter of hours, something having to do with a new law of the land. Everything in the Norton dress shop, too, had turned some shade of green, prom dresses the color of dollar bills or peas. At the adoption agency, that nasty Myrna Lawson grabbed Henry's birth certificate from me, stuck it in the pocket of a green dress she was wearing and ran out the door.

One of those crazy, made up dreams, no willys with it. And the trip to Norton went just fine, plenty of white prom dresses to choose from in my size. At the adoption agency, just to be safe, I kept the birth certificate hidden in my purse, determined to leave with it rather than give it to Myrna. Turned out, she was there and wearing a green dress, which was spooky. But she stayed busy in the back and it was Mrs. Weaver's smiling face that greeted me.

When I handed her the birth certificate she took one look and her eyebrows went up. "Oh, I see. Does Henry know, or his mother?" She was speaking in whispers.

I shook my head. "She asked but I didn't tell her. We both decided the truth should be here in the file, in case Henry gets curious someday. I hope he waits a long, long time, though. Growing up with this, especially around here, won't do a boy any good at all."

"Does *he* know?" she asked.

"That he has a son? Yeah, he's known all along but wants nothing to do with him." Mrs. Weaver didn't seem surprised. She found the file and put the birth certificate inside. It was my turn to whisper. "Any chance it could leak out? Reporters would love it and I worry about the boy."

"No need to worry. We have a code of silence here." She reached in the drawer for a stamp and used it to mark the file, Restricted, in bold red ink. "Just as a precaution, I'll put it in the strongbox with the others we've had to safeguard. Might make you feel better to know it's not our only case involving a famous or infamous parent."

>*>*>*<*<*<

During those long, drawn out months between the arrest and the trial, the Chief fed facts to the newspapers as much as he wanted with little concern for Dollarhide's reputation. I think he enjoyed ripping the guy apart. Up until then, it apparently had not occurred to Betula Bulletin editor, Roland Morgan, to challenge any of Dollarhide's actions, even while people said there was plenty to question.

Yet now it was open season and he was fair game. (Pardon the hunter lingo here but it seems to fit.) Old scores to be settled and a need for revenge, they were all coming out to get satisfied. Dollarhide's crony network seemed to dry up overnight. People barely looked his way anymore, except to throw daggers. He might have fared better driving a less conspicuous car. That Cadillac everybody once admired had become something to resent.

Even his father-in-law spoke out with a cutting comment. "He might be a current member of this family but he's on his own with this one." A *current* member? If I'd been Dollarhide I'd have worried.

Meanwhile, the senator began spending less time in Betula, more time in Richmond, and Canby Kluth requested a bench trial. Dad said it was the smart thing to do, since finding an unbiased jury would be impossible here.

Eighteen

The trial finally began Wednesday, June 11, in Wise, the county seat. Mother and I rode over there with Dad, she in the front, me in the back. We hadn't ridden like that in, what? Nine, ten years? I put up with jumpiness the entire forty-minute ride, mostly because of the trial, I guess, though part of me dreaded ahead of time the scene Mother could make if she wanted.

In the courtroom from the second row, I watched the circuit judge take the bench my grandfather once filled, to preside over this trial where Aunt Clara was the only real witness. Her time had finally come, yet all we had were her words on a page and I waited to see if they'd count. Dad planned to introduce the journal as evidence and put me on the stand to tell the court what she'd said in the hospital.

William Dollarhide sat with his lawyer in a million-dollar suit. I wanted to study him, try to read his mood, but the only decent view I had was of his back. Now and then, when he leaned over to whisper something to Kluth, I saw his profile and it looked full of smirk.

My father appeared smooth and confident wearing his poker face, ponytail and sensible black suit. He held his own just fine with the legendary Canby Kluth. Mother would never admit it, but her face said she was proud. And, why not? He was handsome, professional, not easily riled and, with that ponytail, conspicuous. By the end of the first day, though, the trial still had yet to get started, what with all the delays, motions and objections from the other side.

The next morning I was jumpy again as we crossed over the mountain to Wise, but when you're feeling that way in a steady stream, it's hard to pick out any meaning.

"We have enough time for a quick breakfast this morning, if anyone's interested," Dad said.

"Let's do that," Mother said, "I'm starved."

When we walked into the diner, three men had their heads in a huddle over a newspaper. While Mother and I chose a table, Dad went to a rack, picked up a copy of the Norton Gazette for himself, glanced at the headline and paid for it with a nickel. Then, with the paper folded under an arm, he met us at the table, leaned over and whispered, "We need to leave now, meet me at the car. Sorry, Evelyn." Surprised and worried, we picked up our things and followed. Back at the car he tossed the newspaper to me. "How did this happen?" The headline screamed:

Dollarhide Fathered Illegitimate Child.

"Oh no!" I turned the paper so Mother could see. "Do they give his name?"

"Read for yourself," Dad said. "Read it out loud."

"A reliable unnamed source, in an exclusive interview with the Norton Gazette, said Senator Dollarhide fathered a child out of wedlock. The source refused to identify the name of

146

the mother, or the exact age and identity of the child. This report adds further complications to the Senator's already murky future in light of ..." I quickly scanned the rest of the short article. "Nothing ... no details. Boy, that's a relief!"

"Who do you think did it?"

"I don't know! Nobody knew it but us, and the adoption agency, of course. But Mrs. Weaver assured me it would not get out. She even locked it in a safe in the back room instead of filing it with the others." But, suddenly, I knew. Didn't say anything, but I knew. It had to be Myrna Lawson.

Dad blinked at me. "I think you know. Do you?"

"Maybe, but I need to make a telephone call to be sure."

"It's nearly nine. I better get to the courthouse." He made a move to leave, then hesitated. "This will be in the Bulletin today or tomorrow, and the Richmond papers, too. Kluth will blame us. It might cause a reaction from the judge, so if you have something to tell me ..."

"What kind of reaction?"

"Anger at us, sympathy for the other side."

The adoption agency didn't open until ten. At the diner I ordered breakfast and practiced what to ask while I ate. It wouldn't help to sound accusing. At ten o'clock I traded a dollar for dimes, shut myself into a phonebooth and asked the operator to connect me to the adoption agency. Turned out, I didn't need to ask anything.

"You are calling about the article," Mrs. Weaver offered from the start.

"Yes, this is just awful."

"Grace, I'm deeply sorry. Myrna talked to the reporter. I take full responsibility, this is no place for her. She looks down on parents who abandon their children and has always let it show."

"The article said she didn't name the mother or the child. Is that true?"

"Yes. The mother is gone and she'd never hurt a child. As wrong as her action was, the intent was only to lash out at Dollarhide. I think she hoped to seal his fate in view of his current troubles."

I didn't have the heart to tell her it might backfire. "But the reporter knows the agency is involved. Word will get out. Couldn't somebody just break in and steal the file?"

"I already thought of that. We keep a safe deposit box at the bank. I'm taking the file, all the restricted files, in there today. And just so you know, Myrna resigned. At least that saves me from having to fire her."

I hoofed down the street to the courthouse, surprised to see people pouring out the door and standing in small groups on the steps. I weaved my way up and saw my father still in the courtroom, Mother on a bench in the hall. "What happened?" I asked her. "Recessed already?"

"I'll let your father tell you."

In the privacy of the car, he told me. "Well, predictably, Kluth complained about the article, accused us of releasing the information in order to influence the court. He said it was unsubstantiated information, nothing to do with the case."

Dad rolled down his window and opened the car door. Mother and I did the same because of the heat. "I denied any connection, of course. Then Kluth said the most surprising thing." Dad grinned at Mother and she grinned back. He was pausing for effect, which is unlike him. In fact, he hates when other people do it.

"Well, what did he say?" I asked like he wanted me to.

"Kluth demanded to know how I found out so fast, said a woman came forward just last month claiming Dollarhide had fathered her year-old daughter. He denies it. Kluth assumes she's just looking for quick money. But the woman's angry father apparently threatened to kill Dollarhide and the article just added fuel. Kluth said his side had nothing to gain by talking to the newspapers, so it had to be us."

"Kluth thinks the article is about the other kid?"

"Yep, and it probably is about the other kid."

"No, Dad, it's not." I told him about Myrna Lawson.

"Oh." He started the car without saying anything more, turned out of the parking lot and headed home. A few miles into the trip, he said, "Well, I believe Henry's safe. I doubt Kluth even knows his client fathered a child in 1943. But, the judge is not happy."

"No?"

"On the surface, he's angry about the timing of the article. But underneath, he's assuming an attorney in his court, in the middle of a trial, thought he could be influenced. Judges don't like that. So, he adjourned for the day in a cloud of steam. Hard to predict what will happen next. And, of course, I can't say a word about the actual source without giving it all away." He lit a cigarette and chuckled. "Kluth came up to me afterward and wanted to know how I found out."

"What did you tell him?"

"Nothing, just smiled and let him think what he would. Enjoyed the moment of victory, I gotta admit, though it was only by a stroke of luck and undeserved."

I guess you could say my thoughts were divided going to bed that night, what with the trial and the senior prom the next day. When lightening flashed behind thunderheads in the morning, it gave me prickly willys of the doom variety. My mother got up with a bad headache and decided to stay home. To make matters worse, it was Friday the thirteenth. Mr. Grant says it's silly superstition to be afraid of a particular day, but I don't know.

In court, almost the first thing, Canby Kluth successfully convinced the ill-tempered judge to throw out Aunt Clara's journal on the grounds that, among other things, it referred merely to *a* William without a last name. It was the beginning of the end, you might say. The whole case fizzled a short time later, ceasing with much less notice in the news than before it began. My father said it probably would have ended that way anyhow, even without the article.

I know, I know, there was no conviction. I never got my turn on the stand, we never got to the hat. But in a sense, we achieved what we set out to do. The trial itself, and all the bad newspaper articles, had finished Dollarhide in our town. I bet he couldn't get a job as stock boy at Piggly Wiggly, much less run for a second term in the upcoming election.

From the beginning, we told each other it would be enough. I guess we meant it.

To avoid reporters, my dad made himself scarce after the trial. Canby Kluth, too, managed to escape them by leaving town. He had breezed in nearly a year earlier with a confident spring in his step and departed the same way.

Dollarhide, however, did not avoid reporters. Outside the courthouse they gathered around to ask questions while I leaned against a pillar and watched. "The trial went the only way it could go," he said with a look I'd describe as smug. "It's hard to convict an innocent man in this country. One of the reasons we fought the war was to preserve this kind of protection."

We fought the war? The phony politician had surfaced. He had never fought one day.

"The prosecution had no evidence, only hearsay and conjecture. It was a waste of the court's time."

One of the reporters broke away and came over to me. "Miss Dawson? I'm Harry Greg from the Richmond Times-Dispatch."

"Yes, Mr. Greg, I know who you are."

"I'd like to interview you, if you wouldn't mind." I glanced at my watch and hesitated. He took it as reluctance, I guess. "Please, Miss Dawson. People will be disappointed that you didn't get your chance on the stand. I assume there's more to it than they covered in the trial."

"A fair assumption."

"Readers in the senator's district will want to know, they deserve to know."

Dollarhide adjusted his tie and looked our way.

"I would be happy to talk to you. I do have a lot to say. The problem now is time. My senior prom is tonight, should have left an hour ago." I was thinking of my hair.

"Tomorrow morning, then. I need to make the Sunday edition. How about eleven o'clock at the diner in Betula. Give you time to sleep in," he said, winking.

Dollarhide heard it all, paying more attention to our conversation than his. The smugness was gone, more now like an animal on the prowl, I'd say.

On the way home I told Dad about the interview. "Can I tell him what I want?"

"Sure you can, within reason, but don't think about that now. Just enjoy tonight. You'll only have one senior prom."

I smiled at him and took it to heart, never suspecting Obie and I would miss it.

Nineteen

I spent a whole hour piling hair on my head, entwining white ribbon through it to match my dress. I thought it looked pretty good. Even Mother said so, and praise from her comes scarce. Obie showed up at seven-thirty in a tuxedo and bowtie, shiny as a Christmas present. You should've seen the way he looked at me! He's never been one to whistle at girls but he sure whistled at me that night coming down the stairs. Mother took pictures.

Proms are always held at our high school, only a fifteen-minute ride from my house, on Highway 21. We are not big enough here in Betula to make a good-sized dance on our own, so we invite kids in from Flat Gap and Pound. A few even come from across the Kentucky line.

According to Obie, who'd spent a usual day at school, the Junior Class had taken a stab at turning the gymnasium into a Hawaiian paradise—paper lanterns, grass tree skirts, a giant mural with palm trees and a moon, and those little umbrellas for the punch.

It was just getting dark when we pulled out on the road. Obie was driving my car instead of his truck because of the fancy clothes, and I stayed on my side of the seat instead of scooting to the middle near him.

"What are you doing way over there?" he asked.

"Giving this dress every chance to arrive unwrinkled."

"Well, okay, just this once." After a mile or two he looked in the rearview mirror and frowned.

"What is it?" I asked, shifting to see for myself.

"That car came up awful fast and now it's tailgating." Obie pushed down on the pedal. The car stayed with us, hugging the bumper. "There's two of them in there."

The driver darted into the other lane, came alongside and revved his engine like he wanted to drag race.

"It's a black Dodge, Obie," I said, clutching his arm. With my hair piled up I had nothing to twist, and didn't have any gum.

Obie slowed down hoping they would pass. They slowed, too. He sped up, they sped up. They crowded into our lane! "What the hell?" Obie shouted, gripping the wheel with both hands. We went on that way for must have been a half mile. The two cars, together, squeezed across the Pinefalls bridge. Then, where the land dips down to the creek on my side, they swerved at us again, scraping metal to metal, door handle to door handle!

Obie stood his ground until he couldn't. "They're gonna run us off the road!" he cried, reaching to slam an arm across my chest. They kept at it, forcing us further over, inch by inch. Obie tried to hang on, tried to push back!

I remember leaving the road. The free fall that went on endlessly, scary bumps, lurches, fear we'd flip over careening down where no car ought to go.

Next thing I knew, a hospital bed, both parents leaning over me with big fearful eyes, united in a common concern. My left arm hurt. I looked down to see a nurse busy setting it in a cast. The movement made my head pound. "Where is Obie?" I asked with alarm, remembering.

"Other side of the curtain, honey," Mother said, clutching my free hand. "Don't worry. He's okay."

"Better off than you," Dad said.

A few minutes later, the Chief stepped around the curtain to check on me and deliver a report on his son—a bump on the head and a nasty leg cut. "You two were damned lucky to get out of there with nothing but breaks and cuts."

"What about my car?"

"Needs serious repairs but I don't think it's fatal."

Turned out, the only fatality was my dress, caked in mud and balled up on a chair in the corner. So much for wearing it to graduation. The Chief asked me to tell what I remembered, and I did, making a special point of the black Dodge. "I bet it was those same men, the same ones with the rattlesnakes last summer."

"Did they look familiar?"

"No, never saw them before."

"We hunted that car for months, so I'm quite sure they're not from around here."

"What are we going to do about this, Emmet?" my dad asked. "I've got half a mind to send her away for the summer. You'll go with her, won't you, Evelyn? Maybe to Florida?"

"I certainly will! She's had enough excitement and so have I."

"Eh, it's not that bad" I said. "When we went off the road last night I saw my life flash in front of me, just like people say. It was pretty boring."

"Boring?" Mother said in disbelief. "Rattlesnakes and road accidents, boring?"

"Oh, that was just because of the interview. Dollarhide heard me talking to that reporter and threatened me with his eyes. He was just trying to scare me into not doing it. Hey, what time is it?" With a hand on my aching head I turned to a window and saw dark.

"It's about midnight," Mother said.

"Oh good, I haven't missed it."

"You should not do the interview, Gracie, not after this. Who knows what he'll try next."

"No, Mother, I need to do it! Besides, once it's done it will be too late for him, damage done, cat out of the bag. I'll be safe at that point, won't I, Chief?" I was hoping for an ally. Even my father couldn't be trusted in this.

"No guarantees. The man's vindictive."

I didn't look good—arm in a sling and a battered forehead, but my mouth worked fine. The Chief delivered me to the diner himself the next morning and brought Donnie Ray's hat from the evidence room.

At first, Harry Greg seemed more interested in side issues than the real story. Did I know who ran us off the road, were we responsible for the report that Dollarhide fathered a child, and so on.

But when I told him the tellable part of Aunt Clara's declaration, showed him her journal account of Donnie Ray's death and then came up with the hat, his eyes got big as hit records. I admit it was great fun. This was the kind of impact we'd hoped for in court, but it would never have happened with the journal thrown out. With the journal, the hat was damning evidence. Without the journal, it was just his hat.

Harry Greg's article came out Sunday on the front page of the Richmond Times-Dispatch, including a large photograph of the hat. Dad said my words did more damage in the court of public opinion than any formal testimony could have. In the courtroom, Canby Kluth would have shut me up fast by calling it hearsay.

The Chief found the two men in the black Dodge and arrested them. He admitted to flimsy evidence, locked them up anyhow, said he'd keep them there until the circuit judge came around again, which wouldn't be for a month. I half expected another fancy lawyer to show up and bail them out. When days passed and it didn't happen, Dad figured the senator would let them rot before showing any connection.

After the trial, Dollarhide seemed to spend more time in Betula. This was a surprise, our town being such unfriendly territory for him. But then word spread that, soon after the "fathered a child" article, his fed-up wife kicked him out of the Richmond mansion with plenty of help from daddy, and he was apparently pressured to resign from the state senate before his term was up. Obie said he passed Dollarhide on the street and saw hatred in his eyes.

Twenty

As Graduation approached I begged Mother to be friendly with Dad and not make a scene. Please, oh, please, for my sake. She acted hurt, as though she'd never do such a thing. "I don't see any reason to be friendly, but I'll certainly be civil. I'm always civil," she said. I worried about it until the very day because she was rarely civil to him.

On the morning of the ceremony, Mother drove us to the school in her car because mine was still in getting fixed. We rolled down the front windows in a defense against the heat as she pulled out on Highway 21.

I felt uneasy. To be expected, I told myself, after being run off that same road a few days before. There was nothing to fear, the men in the black Dodge safely locked in the Chief's jail. I gripped the armrest, took a deep breath and let it out slow as the symptoms doubled. I hid them from Mother. The road stretched empty behind us. Ahead, there was one car coming, and another parked on my side of the road, a blue one. I thought it might be Dad with car trouble. But as we got closer, I could see it wasn't him. Mother sped up because she doesn't trust people on the side of a road.

Then, the most shocking thing. A man in the blue car fired a gun at us! He fired a gun! The bullet shattered the window behind me! Mother jammed the gas pedal to the floor and really took off. We were scared to death he'd follow, scared he'd try again. But he didn't, maybe because of the other car passing by. We rocketed straight to the school parking lot and found the Chief.

The principal delayed everything. Nobody minded, which is one advantage to living with small-town folks. They were content to just stand in the shade and speculate about it, tell us how lucky we were.

Turned out, it was Preacher Savage who had passed us on the road and seen the whole thing. He broke into the crowd and described what happened in his booming Sunday voice. Everybody figured the bullet was meant for me. Obie looked angry and white faced about it. Mother felt dizzy and went to sit down. Dad and the Chief left together in the squad car and stayed away for an hour.

After graduation, which I walked through in a fog and barely remember, we stood around some more, nibbled on brownies and sipped a tasty punch made from orange juice and ginger ale.

Dad was obviously still thinking about sending me away for the summer. I heard him discuss it with the Chief. "I'm afraid Dollarhide blames my daughter for his entire decline."

"Sure seems like it," the Chief said.

"Isn't there something we can do?"

"Damned if I know, offhand. When you've got ants eating your picnic, you can chase them away all you want. But the truth is, you eventually need do something about the anthill."

160

Ernie Reed caught the man in the blue car, pulled him over heading to Pound on Route 671. The Chief called us in later to identify the man. Mother and I, neither one, could say for sure, but luckily the preacher could.

>*>*>*<*<*<

There is something wonderful and painful about closing the door on high school. I lazed around the house for two whole days and became quite sentimental on the subject. But on the third day, back again in my father's law office, I saw it as natural and necessary, like being born. I tried to get Dad to take me out to lunch. Not a long lunch, just a quick hotdog at Jerky's.

"Don't have the time, Gracie," he mumbled from behind a stack of lawbooks. "You go without me. And bring me one back."

"Mustard and onions?"

"Yeah. Actually, make it two." He had recently agreed to prosecute a man accused of manslaughter, and there was hard evidence in this case. He didn't say he needed a win after the fiasco with Dollarhide but I knew he felt it. So, he was stirred into action, hunkered down, going great guns. We were busy, plenty to do, is my point. In fact, the lunch at Jerky's was my last going out for a while. I'm telling you this now to squelch any notion that too much idle time triggered an overactive imagination, which is what Mother has always said about my premonitions.

This will be shocking and hard to believe, dear reader, but I am fairly certain William Dollarhide is lying dead at the bottom of the break. I know, I know, but listen. First thing, nobody's seen him for a week. Second, plenty around here wanted him gone. Third, nobody's curious where he went or even wonders if he's missing, including the Chief. It's like they already know.

Fourth, and most important, a vivid dream that gave me a deep case of the willys. I awoke with a jerk to images of men with hushed voices carrying something heavy to the edge of the break and hurling it over the side. Clear, solid images right down to the crush of boots on dry leaves, snap of branches as it fell, and a muffled thud in the quiet of the night when it hit bottom way down. Then, silence. Something long like a body, wrapped in an old blanket and tied with rope, now lying crooked in a shallow grave between a scraggly dogwood and an aging cedar.

It made me pop out of bed like a piece of Dad's toast. It's Dollarhide's body, I know it! It's an inner knowing, and it's strong, stronger than walking into the ransacked house and you know how that turned out.

>*>*>*<*<*<

We moved Henry and his mother to Smoketown Road last week. Mary Mullin said she would be honored to live there and keep the house nice. A privilege, she said, to dust such fine furniture and cook in such a kitchen. Then, Silas asked if there might be a need for his wife to help with the inside chores. I asked if they both wanted, for convenience, to live in the caretaker's cottage. He laughed out loud and slapped his knee and said they certainly would! Well, okay, then.

The whole thing felt right. I taught Henry to wind all five clocks, how to adjust the time, if necessary, when the fire department blows its whistle at noon. He's a capable boy. Aunt Clara would be proud.

Buster did a job on the neighbor's dog next door and a litter of pups appeared. There's nothing cuter than a hound-dog pup. Obie will take one as soon as they are weaned, and there's talk of giving one to Henry.

As for Obie and me, looking back, we have both developed a fierce fondness for mystery, half sorry now that this one is at an end. Come fall, we are supposed to leave for college. Obie still doesn't want to go. He tried putting his size eleven foot down about it but the Chief stomped on it with his size twelve. Then, Obie's mother got involved and they settled on the state police academy if Obie can get in, and I know he can.

When I leave, his class ring will stay in a drawer here at home. We talked about it and he agrees. It's so much a part of high school, too juvenile for college. Plus, Obie hasn't said anything yet, but I am expecting an engagement ring soon.

Twenty-One

Dollarhide is still missing. Yet, nobody's asking questions, not the family or anybody else. Don't you find it odd? The longer he is missing, the truer my dream will feel. If I tell people, they won't believe me. I can't prove it, so I'd have to say it's just a feeling. And even if they did believe me, who would care enough to go down there and find out. My dad would believe but I think I'll spare him. Sometimes, just like with the birth certificate, knowing can be a burden. And I'll spare the Chief and Obie, too. I mean, what if the Chief was involved? I can't say for sure who threw Dollarhide down the break. The truth is, I don't want to know.

Will I have the need for a deathbed declaration of my own one day? I doubt it. I don't really *know* anything, not in a legal sense. All I had was a dream and a bad case of the willys. One day, folks will begin to talk. Then they'll decide the mountains took him as a rounding out of justice. Once they get into that territory, what I'd say would just confirm it. In the meantime, still, nobody's asking where he went, nobody seems to care.

We spent the whole of yesterday on Smoketown Road. I sat next to Mary in the parlor and watched Obie and Henry roughhouse with Buster and the pups. Obie dipped back to nine years old. Together, they laughed out loud and rolled and tumbled and tickled each other and laughed some more until they knocked a lamp off a table and Henry went on a coughing jag. Mary chased the dogs outside and sat Henry on the couch to settle down with a glass of water.

She seemed embarrassed by the uproar. I thought it was wonderful. "Mary, this house has known nothing but sadness over the years. I bet it's the happiest day these poor old walls ever had."

"You know what? From now on, things are going to be right as rain. I can feel it," Obie added, catching the mood.

Don't know about that, but things are certainly fine at the moment and they will continue to be fine until they're not. Mother says the future seldom unfolds the way we expect. Will we be happy the rest of our lives? Will Obie ever stray? Will our children look up to us when they are older or think we're just a couple of dopes. There's such a wideness to the world. Maybe it would help to strike a solid pose right now and demand it to turn our way.

I know Dollarhide is gone. Sometimes, you just know things. Tomorrow is a guess but at least I'm sure the sun will come up in the morning, Mother and I will have our break-fast and I'll wind the clocks for her one last time before I go. All is right with the world, as they say, at least for now.

In my mind, justice has been served. But, dear reader, I'll leave it for you to decide.

Turn the page for an excerpt from
"The Roommate"
Book Two of the Grace Dawson Series
now available on Amazon in print or Ebook

THE
ROOMMATE

Grace Dawson Series: Book Two

K. J. MCCALL

One

Grace Dawson   August, 1952

It rained the day I left for Stapleton College. The night before that I dreamt of crickets and then stepped on one in the early-morning dark, the poor thing's innards oozing between my toes, wet and cold. It felt like an omen, that and the rain.

It wouldn't be exaggerating to say plenty happened my first college year. Not so much to me. Mostly, I just watched other people, warned myself not to get involved and paid for it when I did. To begin with, two women my same age disappeared, each on her own steam and for her own good reason. But I'm racing ahead.

The whole thing started with voices on the train. In the last hour of the five-hour ride from Betula, Virginia, a couple got on and took the seat behind me. I barely noticed at first, thumbing through a *Sears Roebuck* catalog that somebody had left on the seat. And it was not my plan to listen. But then the woman asked, "What are we going to do?" and she said it with tears.

"Maybe he's wrong. Have you thought of that?" This from a man with a radio voice.

"How could he be wrong, George? He's a doctor."

Well, a conversation like that could only mean one thing, and I admit to listening on purpose, then. Nothing else was said, though, for maybe a minute. Calculated coddling, I figured.

He finally said, "Honey, I'm so sorry."

"You keep saying that but what are we going to do?"

"You keep asking that and I'm telling you I don't have an answer yet. Just found out an hour ago."

"Tell me you love me."

"I *love* you," he offered in a silky tone.

"Enough to get a divorce and marry me? You said you don't love her."

Uh-oh. I knew right then that it wouldn't end well for her.

"I can't do that. At least, not now."

"When?"

"Sometime, but it can't be now."

"It's got to be soon or it won't do any good."

"I'm so sorry, really I am."

"What should I do?" She sounded pitiful.

"We'll think of something but please don't cry, you'll draw attention. Radford is the next stop and I need to get off."

"Can't I come with you?" So, so pitiful.

170

"Please, don't ask that. You know we can't go back to-gether."

"Just this once?"

"What if somebody sees? How would we ever explain?"

"But, I'm scared. And if you're getting a divorce, why does it matter?"

"Now I'm scared, hearing you talk like that. I'll meet you next Friday, as usual. We'll talk it all over and ... chin up until then."

I gave the man a good stare as he passed on the way out. Tall and tan, definitely above average in the looks department, good enough to model suits in the *Sears Roebuck* catalog.

I heard her sniffle and blow her nose for the next half hour until the train pulled into Roanoke where we both got off. Just as I had figured—nineteen more or less, blond and pretty. Isn't that how it always goes. He was probably thirty and too handsome for anybody's good. I locked eyes with her and tried to paint my face with sympathy. I must've succeeded because she reacted with fear, knowing I'd heard. With a slow blink and tiny nod I promised to keep mum. She looked relieved and thanked me with a woeful smile. A lot got said in that two-second silent conversation.

We both caught the bus to Stapleton, which made me wonder if she was a college student, too. Then, I heard my father's firm voice telling me to stay out of other folks' affairs. In Stapleton, I treated myself and my suitcase to a taxicab from the bus station, lost track of the woman in the process.

Stapleton College had appeared lovely and dignified in pictures they had sent—solid brick buildings, chunky white pillars, stretches of green lawn dotted with happy-looking students. The real thing did not disappoint. The taxi driver dropped me near the registrar's office. I paid him and got out. Clusters of students stood around. I assumed they were all first years, since it was Friday, move-in day for freshmen and the start of orientation. The upperclassmen weren't due until Sunday.

Next to the sidewalk ahead, in the shade of a tree, a couple stood talking. Well, it was mostly the guy talking, and in a menacing sort of way. A muscly type, bristly brown crewcut and a squared-off chin. Certainly not a freshman, more like a senior, and on the football team. Since I was going to pass right by them, I prepared to smile.

He reached up and put an open hand on her head in a gesture that seemed almost sweet, but then he grabbed a handful of hair and yanked her head back. Just as I got within hearing distance, he said in a nasty whisper, "I'm the one who controls things around here. I tell you what to do and you do it!" A real charmer, this guy.

Whoever the girl was, she looked easy to push around, a scared rabbit, frail and timid. She stood with her back to me so I couldn't see her face, but she was cowering. Then he whispered something else that only she could hear. Whatever it was caused her to whimper, which raised the hair on my arms. He glared at me and let her go. "I just don't like the idea of you working in the diner, is all," he said mildly.

After that little scene and the one on the train, I was not impressed with the men around there, and had to remind myself again to stay out of other folks' business. But it didn't hurt to wonder.

I had never been this far from home before. The furthest I'd been from Betula was Norton, forty-five minutes away. My mother wanted me to attend Radford State Teachers' College for Women, where Sears Roebuck had apparently parked his car. My Aunt Clara had gone there to get her teaching degree, and Mother just assumed I'd follow. When I picked Stapleton, she said I did it just to be contrary but that wasn't the reason, not the main one anyway. First, I want a law degree, not a teaching degree. And second, Radford is a women's college and I want coed. Not that I'm looking, mind you, even if it turns out that Stapleton is a dreamboat capitol. I already have a boyfriend, Obie Sayer, the Betula police chief's son. No engagement ring on my finger yet but it's just a matter of time. That boy can light up a rainy day for me.

The registrar gave me a dormitory assignment, a class schedule, and put two keys in my hand. "The big one is to your room, the tiny one is the key to your letter box. Don't lose them. Replacements will cost you fifty cents."

I nodded and clicked them into my coin purse. I didn't intend to lose either of them. Letter writing was to be my main connection with home—Mother, Dad, and especially Obie, who'd left Betula the day before wearing a baseball cap and a grin, heading to Richmond to try for the state police academy. He would write me from there and we planned to splurge once a week on a telephone call. "Oh, are there telephones?" I rushed to ask.

"There's one on each dormitory floor and several in the student union outside the dining hall. You will need a lot of coins for a long-distance call, though, unless you reverse the charges."

My room was in the freshman dormitory, Harrison Hall, the oldest on campus. I met Mrs. Gordy, the housemother, on the way in. She seemed the soft and gentle type, sort of grandmotherly. "You're Grace Dawson?"

"Yes, ma'am," I said, polite-like.

"Third floor, room 314. You have a roommate, Miss Penny Thayer. She's already moved in."

"Thank you. Up there?" I asked, pointing to the stairs. Stupid. Where else would the third floor be? Well, I was nervous.

She nodded with a tolerant smile. "Just go up and turn to the right. Number's on the door. Have you read the *Rules of Conduct*, Miss Dawson?"

"Yes, ma'am," I said, glad it was the truth.

"What time is curfew?"

"Midnight Saturdays, ten the rest of the time."

"Good, and that means in your room, which makes the telephone off limits after curfew, as well."

"Yes, ma'am."

"You can come to me with problems, day or night. Even after curfew, if necessary. My apartment is right here." She pointed to the room by the double front doors I had just entered.

Lugging my suitcase up the two flights of stairs, I prepared to meet my roommate. Penny Thayer, nice name. I hoped we'd be fast friends. She wasn't in there but she'd already claimed the right side of the room by putting her suitcase on the bed. So, I took the left.

It was a big room for two people, with a high ceiling and two nice windows looking out on the lawn. The trunk I'd shipped two weeks earlier had arrived, with everything I might need until Thanksgiving, including a winter coat and snow boots.

The college had sent out information in a packet, all about the school and the *Rules of Conduct*, which spelled out what all we could do and not do. On the subject of dress, it had a lot to say. Pants and shorts were not permitted on campus, except just long enough to come and go. We could go to Lake Lorraine in pants or shorts and wear a bathing suit underneath, but we were not allowed to remove those clothes until we got there. The rules said we needed white gloves for the President's Tea and other possible occasions during the year. Nothing was said about a hat requirement, but gloves and hats went together in Betula so I had packed two, a brown felt for cold weather and a yellow straw for warm.

One thing was good. We could chew gum here, even in class, something we were never permitted to do in high school. My favorite is Doublemint but I settle for any kind in a pinch.

I found a place for everything, filling the four-drawer bureau on my side of the room, and half the closet. I set out toiletries on the top of my bureau and looked in the mirror to examine what felt like a pimple popping on my chin.

That's when she showed up, my roommate. You probably assumed she was one of the women I mentioned, either the scared rabbit or the one on the train. She was the scared rabbit. I stumbled over my surprise in order to be extra friendly, since meeting one's roommate for the first time seemed an important event. But she just gave me a weak hello and settled at her desk chair with her back to me. I figured she was just upset and she'd show me a friendly side later.

She certainly had reason to be upset but seemed to be handling it well. Me? I'd be curled up in a ball after a run-in like that. She probably didn't know I had witnessed the whole scene. Had she told anybody? I would be fleeing to Mrs. Gordy and the police.

Sneaking glances at her, the words that came to mind were pale and frail. Milky skin, limp, light hair in her face. Looked as though she never ate and could be blown down the street in a wind. We didn't look a thing alike. My dark hair to her blond, and I had her by a few pounds. Also, she was a nail biter, a habit I'd left behind.

At dinner time I suggested we walk to the dining hall together. She said no thanks, so we each went over alone, which seemed rather silly. On purpose, I took a seat at a table that was almost full, hoping to make some friends. I searched around for Penny and didn't see her at first, until the dining hall workers brought in the food. There she was, doing a decent job of balancing a tray too big for her. So that meant she was working to swing the tuition. Nothing unusual about that. Lots of students probably needed help. In contrast, I didn't know what a money shortage felt like.

I recommend selecting a table with the idea of making friends, because I met Steve and Lily that evening at dinner. They'd known each other outside of school, already having that easy familiarity, and they welcomed me into it. At one point, the table started talking about roommates and we all agreed it was nerve-wracking business, like wondering what hand you'll be dealt in a big card game. Steve seemed to approve of his so far and Lily didn't have one yet. I kept quiet about mine and nobody asked.

It was still light outside when I got back to the dorm at eight. Penny walked in at 9:59, cutting it close to curfew. I had trouble going to sleep that night, both of us lying there with faces to the wall, so unfriendly-like. I considered asking to switch rooms, maybe move in with Lily, but it didn't feel right to give up on Penny yet.

Who was the bristly-headed guy? That's what I wanted to know. He was obviously the problem. I assumed it was her boyfriend, but of course I couldn't ask. I wanted her to confide in me but since she wasn't even talking, we were a long way from that. I wondered if Mrs. Gordy knew. She seemed the type to not miss much.

On Saturday I asked Penny if she wanted to walk around campus, find all our classes ahead of time. She said she couldn't so I went alone. That evening at dinner, the Dean of Students gave a little welcoming speech and reminded us of President Beard's Freshman Tea at two the next day, an annual event.

On Sunday morning I skipped breakfast and church in order to sleep in, a routine I'd soon perfect. Penny did the same. She still hadn't said more than a half-dozen words. My oh my, it was going to be a lonely year in room 314.

We dressed for the President's Tea at the same time, silently moving around each other. I liked her tailored dress and told her so. Her hair, however. It was always hanging in front of her eyes, I wondered how she could see. My mother liked to brush the bangs away from my face and I felt the same urge here. Or better still, find some scissors. Did neither, of course, just reached in a bureau drawer for a spare barrette and said, "This one's an extra if you want it."

Then I opened the door to leave and nodded at her bare hands. "They said we have to wear white gloves for this thing."

She just shrugged.

"You don't have any?"

Another shrug.

I went back to my bureau for an extra pair and handed them to her. She pulled them on with a whispered thank you. They were a definite improvement, hiding a worn-out band-aid covering the fingernail she'd chewed raw.

We walked over to Stuart Hall for the reception. At least we did that much together. A long receiving line had already formed and we got in it. Turned out they were serious about the white gloves for women. We watched two surprised coeds get chased out of line because they didn't have any, and I think their names got written down on a pad. Penny looked at her gloved hands and then at me, her mouth curved into something resembling a smile.

Men didn't need gloves, we noticed, and women had to wear them only to shake the president's hand. It was permissible afterwards to remove them for the tea and cookies. I stood with Penny a few minutes out of respect for our roommate arrangement, but soon drifted away in the direction of Steve and Lily.

I had kept an eye out all of Saturday for the girl on the train, still assuming she was a Stapleton student. And I'd wondered on and off about Mr. Sears Roebuck—who he was and where they'd met. Turned out, I didn't have to wonder any longer, not about him anyway. While I was standing there, the crowd shifted a bit and I saw that handsome cheater talking to President Beard. He sure looked like Somebody, a hand on the president's shoulder and wearing an easy smile.

Steve waved a hand in front of my face. "You seem spellbound, Grace. What are you staring at?"

"Who's the man with the president?"

"Ah, I might have known. He's Professor Logan. Every-one notices him, at least everyone in a skirt."

"What's his first name?"

"I bet Lily knows."

"It's George," Lily answered.

"Gosh! He's a professor here?" I'm fairly certain my eyebrows shot up.

"Why are you so surprised? Aren't professors allowed to be handsome?" Lily asked.

"Just like to know who everybody is," I said, realizing I'd shown too much interest.

"I see," Steve said kiddingly. "We've got professors all around this room. Want to know their names, too? How about the bald one over there? He could be mistaken for General Eisenhower."

"Don't tease her, Steve." Lily bopped Steve on the arm. "Grace is simply showing her good taste in men."

"He's handsome, you gotta admit," I said, pretending an interest the same as the rest.

"Well, never fear. You'll be seeing plenty of him," Steve said. "He teaches English Lit to first years, your typical fox in the henhouse. But you need to know he has a handsome wife. Actually, I'm surprised she isn't here today. They say she tries to keep him on a shortened leash."

"You know a lot for someone who just got here. Why is that?" I asked, hoping to send the talk somewhere else.

"My brother's a senior, captain of the basketball team. Gary Fraser, a name you'll hear a lot once the season starts. Women go nuts over him, too. He got the looks and the height in our family, which left me with short and smart."

I smiled at that and thought even better of Steve, so willing to point out his own flaws. He *was* short, no taller than Lily. In fact, head to head, it looked like Lily had an inch on him.

I lost track of Penny and later walked back to the dorm alone, which gave me time to think. Well, the wife's short leash wasn't working. I felt sorry for her and wondered if she knew about the girl. Did anybody else know, or only me.

Sure enough, the next day, Professor Logan stood in front of my English Literature class. I was able to scrutinize the cheater for an entire hour without being obvious, and in the next couple weeks I found myself wondering what his lines of right and wrong looked like. I think he read me as more eager than most, the way I followed him around the room with my eyes. In truth, I was eager about literature, devouring

Great Expectations in high school while everyone else groaned, and now finding *Crime and Punishment* a fascinating read, except for the tangle of Russian names that all sounded the same. Penny was in that class, too, slumped in a back-row seat with hair in her eyes. Maybe the hair helped her hide. Being freshmen, we took mostly the same classes but shared only two, this one and Algebra. I hadn't told her about Professor Logan. I hadn't told anyone.

Books by K.J. McCall

Set Apart 2010
Eighteen in 1942 2014